A Compromising Situation That Isn't What It Seems...

"Stop this indecent behavior at once!" Claire's father shouted.

They stopped and turned their attention to the veranda where a group of people rushed outside to see what caused the commotion. It took Claire a moment to realize how bad the situation looked. Her dress was up to her knees and the gentleman's hands were on her arms. Neither one of them moved for a whole five seconds, and then something snapped and she managed to shove him away. At what was less than a graceful movement, she managed to get to her feet and brushed the lower half of her dress down so she was decent.

"This isn't what it looks like," the gentleman told the crowd. "I was trying to escort her back inside when she tripped and fell onto the grass."

Her sister walked up to their father, a knowing smile on her face. "A likely story."

"It's true," Claire spoke up despite the heat rising up in her cheeks. Truly, she couldn't recall a time when she'd been more humiliated in her life. "I was dizzy."

"Dizzy from lust, no doubt," Lord Edon mumbled, causing a few giggles from the crowd.

An older lady gave him a sharp look. "I won't tolerate that kind of talk here, Lord Edon."

"My apologies, Lady Cadwalader," Lord Edon replied, sounding appropriately contrite.

Claire's father turned his attention back to Claire and the gentleman standing next to her. "I trust your little tryst will lead to a wedding."

Claire's eyes grew wide. A wedding? She glanced at the gentleman. It gave her slight comfort to know he was as stunned as she was. Clearing her throat, she ventured, "It was an accident. We weren't..." She struggled to find the right words, but they evaded her.

Lady Cadwalader shook her head. "Don't let Lord Roderick get away with it, Miss."

Get away with it? But there was nothing to get away with!

Lord Roderick sighed, his shoulders slouched.

Lady Cadwalader motioned to everyone to go back inside. "I didn't plan this evening's ball to spend all of my time outside. Lord Roderick, I assume you'll bring her in for a dance?"

Her father nodded to Lady Cadwalader. "I'll make sure he does right by my daughter."

The

The Earl's Inconvenient Wife

Ruth Ann Nordin

Dedication: To Judy DeVries whose enthusiasm and love for life inspires me to look at the glass as half-full instead of half-empty.

Other Books Written by Ruth Ann Nordin

<u>Regency Collection</u>
The Earl's Inconvenient Wife
Her Counterfeit Husband (coming soon)

<u>Nebraska Historical Romance Collection</u>
Wagon Trail Bride (coming soon)
Her Heart's Desire
A Bride for Tom
A Husband for Margaret
Eye of the Beholder
The Wrong Husband
Shotgun Groom
To Have and To Hold
His Redeeming Bride
Isaac's Decision

<u>South Dakota Historical Romance Series</u>
Loving Eliza
Bid for a Bride
Bride of Second Chances

<u>Native American Romance Series</u> (historical)
Restoring Hope
Brave Beginnings
Bound by Honor, Bound by Love (coming soon)
A Chance In Time (novella) – main characters show up in Restoring Hope and Bound by Honor, Bound by Love)

<u>Virginia Brides Series</u> (historical)
An Unlikely Place for Love
The Cold Wife
An Inconvenient Marriage
Romancing Adrienne

<u>Other Historical Western Romances</u>
Falling In Love With Her Husband
Meant To Be

<u>Contemporary Romances</u>
With This Ring, I Thee Dread
What Nathan Wants
Suddenly a Bride

<u>Christian Sci-Fi Thriller</u>
Return of the Aliens

Chapter One

April 1813
London

"Remind me why I'm here," Nathaniel Buford, Earl of Roderick, said as he checked his gold pocket watch.

Perry Ambrose, Earl of Clement, shook his head in amusement. "I did that exactly forty seconds ago. The answer won't change just because you want it to."

With a sigh, Nate returned the watch to his pocket and looked out the carriage window, noting the crowded streets where horses pulled other carriages toward the same place: Rendell Hall. All the ladies would be dressed in their finest in hopes of snaring a gentleman—preferably one who was titled—to marry. The knot in his stomach tightened. How he hated the marriage market!

"Remind me, again, why I'm here," Nate repeated.

Perry groaned, though a chuckle rose up in his throat. "You poor, poor man. You really should murder your brother for dying without an heir."

"Don't think the thought hasn't crossed my mind." Despite his sour mood, his friend's words made him smile. If anyone could make him feel better about his current predicament, it was his childhood friend, Perry.

"You should count your blessings, Nate. You'll have your pick of ladies."

Their carriage came to a stop, and Nate straightened in his seat. One glance out the window notified him they had reached their destination. Hopeful young ladies who were there to enjoy their Season climbed the stairs to Rendell Hall. Heaven help the ones who were going in for a third Season. They'd probably be better off giving up. Not that such matters concerned him. He was here to get a wife, and with any luck, he'd find her before the night was up.

He glanced at his friend who grabbed his cane. It was ironic that Perry wanted to get married but hadn't had much luck. Between the two of them, Perry was far more jovial. But for some reason, Perry hadn't found a wife, though he'd attended social gatherings in the previous two Seasons. Perry had wagered that Nate would walk out with one before the night was over because, as Perry put it, once Nate set his mind to something, he didn't stop until he got it.

"Try a more congenial countenance, Nate," Perry said as the coachman opened the carriage door. "Ladies prefer gentlemen who smile." Nate forced a smile, and his friend rolled his eyes. "Good heavens. You look like you're in a great deal of pain."

It was close enough to the truth so he didn't deny it. He left the carriage first and breathed in the night air. Somewhere in Rendell Hall was the future Lady Roderick, the lady who'd enable him to pass on the title to his son. That shouldn't be too hard. It would have been preferable if Hester hadn't jilted him so she could marry the Duke of Aquilla, but he doubted she would have been content with being a countess when she could be a duchess instead. When it all came down to it, the title availed much to gentlemen.

His friend steadied himself with his cane and limped over to him. "Don't compare those ladies to Hester."

Surprised, Nate furrowed his eyebrows. "How did you know I was thinking of her?"

With a shrug, he mused, "You grimace when you think of her."

"Do I?"

"I'm afraid so."

Steeling his resolve, he trudged up the steps, going slower than he needed to so that Perry could keep up with him. Having been born with one leg shorter than the other, Perry lacked the grace and speed of other gentlemen.

"It is unfortunate we can't trade places," Nate mumbled as they approached the entrance of the ballroom.

"You don't want to trade places with me," Perry replied as he followed Nate inside. "Might I suggest you pick a lady who is beautiful?"

Lowering his voice so others couldn't hear them, he asked, "You suggest no other attribute?"

"I'm not sure you need another one. Should she be as horrible as you fear, you'd have the consolation of knowing she's nice to look at."

Nate chuckled. Leave it to Perry to find something worth joking about when Nate faced a decision that would affect the rest of his life. Turning his attention to the mission at hand, he scanned the room, noting the couples dancing, some in merriment while others looked as happy to be there as he was. Maybe it was wrong, but he took a small comfort in knowing he wasn't the only bachelor being forced to think of his legacy.

Perry nudged his arm. "What about her?"

His gaze went to the pretty blonde on the other side of the room who fiddled with her curls. "No."

"Why not? She's the best looking lady in the room."

"And she knows it."

Nate watched as a gentleman approached her. She listened as he talked to her, offering him a polite smile. When he was done, she shook her head in dismissal, and the disappointed gentleman walked away. Now he knew why she didn't have a dance partner. She was turning down the offers she was receiving.

"That over there is a vain lady," he told Perry.

"With her beauty, she has a right to be," his friend replied. "You're handsome. She'll say yes to you."

Given that he had no interest in her, he ignored the comment and continued scanning the room to see if a potential Lady Roderick was lurking somewhere. He didn't see anyone who stood out. Oh, there were attractive ladies, but he didn't feel that certain spark he had expected to feel when he laid eyes on the one meant for him.

"There is another way to make your choice," Perry said, drawing Nate's attention back to him. "You could marry someone from a notable family."

Nate's eyebrows rose in surprise. "Why, Perry, I believe you are smarter than you look after all."

With a mock bow, he replied, "You flatter me, my lord."

Chuckling, he switched his attention to the fathers in the room, trying to decide which ones might be the ideal father-in-law. "I suppose I ought to get to work. The right lady won't come to me. I must go to her, and with any luck, her father will point me in her direction."

Nate stepped further into the room, making sure he didn't intrude on the dancing couples. Soon enough, he'd be dancing and talking to ladies whose fathers he got along with. His friend was right. If he could be on good terms with the lady's family, then his life would be easier. Spotting some older gentlemen, he headed for them, determined to find out if they had any daughters.

***

Claire Lowell pulled her white gloves up to her elbows and then brushed off the imaginary lint on her pink evening gown.

"Stop fussing," her sister admonished as she scanned the people who were dancing.

"Forgive me, Lilly." She straightened up and forced her hands at her sides.

"You needn't be so worried."

"This is my first Season. How can I not worry?" Claire asked, taking in all the ladies who exuded far more confidence than she felt. How did they do it? They were calm and poised, speaking smoothly and laughing. They seemed to be enjoying themselves while she...while she felt as if she was going to be sick. "I don't feel well."

Lilly shook her head. "There's nothing to it. I survived my first Season, and you'll survive yours, too."

It was true. Lilly made her rounds to the balls last Season and reported her dance card quite full. "You should have danced with the gentleman who asked you instead of staying with me."

Lilly twirled her blonde strands around her fingers. "Mister Morris might have money, but he doesn't have a title. I don't care how much he pursues me. I won't marry a gentleman unless he has something to offer me."

"Even if it's love? Mister Morris adores you."

She shrugged. "A mere infatuation. Nothing more."

"I think it's rather sweet the way he talks to you."

"Sweet won't make me comfortable for the rest of my life."

"I doubt all the servants and clothes in the world can be sufficient when your husband doesn't love you," Claire whispered.

Lilly laughed as she studied the gentlemen as the dance came to an end. "That's why ladies take lovers once they provide their husband with an heir. You don't need to worry about me."

She resisted the urge to roll her eyes. She wasn't so naïve that she didn't understand the manner in which most of the noble class conducted their personal affairs.

Her gaze swept the room, noting the cordial manner in which people conducted themselves. She had to admit the dancing looked like fun, and part of her wanted to join, even if it meant some degree of embarrassment since she wasn't sure the dancing lessons had paid off. She suspected her unease came more from how she compared to Lilly. Lilly was graceful on her feet and able to keep pace with the steps to the English country-dance. Claire had almost tripped on her way down the end of the line during the last one she'd participated in. She much preferred the waltz, though she did wonder if she hurt her dance partner since she stepped on his foot twice. She cringed at the memory. No. He wouldn't dare venture her way again.

Their mother came over to them with an excited smile. "Your father is coming over here with a suitable bachelor. I do believe he has a title."

Lilly's face lit up and she fluffed her blonde curls. Claire thought about doing something to make her dark hair more attractive but decided there wasn't much she could do when it was piled up on her head with decorative pins in it. Besides, he most likely would want to dance with Lilly anyway.

Her father approached them with a gentleman, and Claire's eyes went to the gentleman's cane. She wondered what might have caused him to need it. A war injury perhaps? He looked young. Perhaps he was in his early twenties. He was good looking with brown hair, a solid frame, and pleasant blue eyes that twinkled with a sense of mirth. Her interest piqued, she focused on her father as he made the introductions.

"This is Lord Clement," he told them before turning back to the gentleman. "These are my daughters, Miss Lilly and Claire Lowell."

Claire and Lilly curtsied, and Lord Clement bowed. "It's a pleasure to meet you," he greeted. "I trust you're finding London to your liking?"

Lilly glanced at Claire, and it took Claire a moment to realize her usually outspoken sister had decided this gentleman wasn't one she wanted so she felt no need to encourage him to talk to her. Clearing her throat, Claire replied, "London is…big, my lord." Her cheeks grew warm. That didn't come out quite right.

Her mother laughed and clapped her hands. "You'll have to forgive my daughters. While Lilly attended the Season last year, this is Claire's first time in London. She finds it overwhelming."

"That's understandable," Lord Clement said. "One hardly sleeps with all there is to do, especially this time of year."

Appreciative of his gracious reply, Claire relaxed. "I haven't seen much of it yet."

"I'm afraid we've been keeping the girls occupied with getting ready for the balls," their father said. "We should do something of interest while we're here."

"Yes, we should," their mother quickly agreed. "What do you suggest, Lord Clement?"

"If they enjoy a circus," he began, "then I suggest Astley's Royal Amphitheatre. However, if they wish to engage with others in London, Hyde Park is a good place to take a walk or ride a horse." He motioned to his cane. "I prefer riding a horse. I have access to a couple of horses if the situation calls for it."

Their father shot their mother an excited look.

"Both activities sound lovely," their mother said, her head bobbing up and down. "We would be remiss if we didn't engage in them while we're here. That would be lovely, wouldn't it?" she asked her daughters.

"Yes, it would," Claire admitted, thinking that Lord Clement was a likable gentleman. One, perhaps, she could even be happy marrying if he was as nice as he seemed.

Lilly bit her lower lip and breathed a sigh of relief when Mister Morris headed their way, his eyes flitting between her and

Lord Clement. When he reached them, he bowed. They returned the greeting and exchanged pleasantries.

Mister Morris stepped over to Lilly in an apparent move to claim the lady he loved. Claire bit her lip so she wouldn't chuckle. If her sister was smart, she'd marry him. She had no doubt he'd be devoted to her every day of his life.

"Might I have the honor of having the next dance?" he asked Lilly.

To Claire's surprise, Lilly gave a quick nod and joined him so they could dance the next waltz. She resisted the urge to shake her head in amazement. Was that the same lady who just claimed she didn't want to be with him? Whatever changed her mind in such a hurry?

"I'm afraid I cannot offer you a dance," Lord Clement said, bringing Claire's attention back to him. He motioned to his cane and shrugged. "I wouldn't be too graceful."

Her mother waved her hand dismissively. "A gentleman's worth isn't based on how he dances but on who he is, right Claire?"

Despite her embarrassment to being singled out, Claire nodded. "Of course, I don't mind."

"She's a wonderful young lady," her father quickly added. "She likes to draw, keeps a record of her thoughts, and has been instructed in how to be a good wife. I even set aside a sizable dowry on her behalf."

Her face flushed. She knew her father meant well, but she felt as if she were an animal up for sale. But perhaps that was what the Season was all about. Her father had wished to see her married well, which was why he saved as much as he did while denying himself some of the finer things in life. Still, she wished he could have chosen other words to express why Lord Clement might consider her for marriage.

As Lord Clement opened his mouth to speak, a gentleman ran over to him. "I'm sorry to disturb you, my lord, but your ward has been caught in a situation that demands your attention at once."

A slight frown crossed his face, but he turned back to her and smiled. "Please accept my apologies. I'm responsible for my cousin. Perhaps I can pay you a visit sometime?"

"Most certainly," her father spoke before she had the chance.

Her father told him where they were staying while in London for the Season, and she wondered if Lord Clement was being polite or if he would, in fact, pay them a visit.

As he limped away, her mother chuckled and gave her arm a light squeeze. "I believe you just might do well this Season."

"A fine match," her father agreed, his chest puffed up with pride.

Her mother scanned the people in the room and told her father, "While the situation with Lord Clement is promising, perhaps we'd do well to find other notable gentlemen who might take an interest in Claire?"

Her father nodded. "Having your pick of gentlemen would be to your advantage," he told his daughter.

Claire hid her disappointment. She'd hoped that this would be the extent of how many gentlemen she was expected to interact with during her Season. Her stomach tensed into knots as her parents discussed possible matches, and she was, once again, fiddling with her gloves.

Her father looked at Claire in excitement. "I think I have a possible match for you." Before she could even see the gentleman he had in mind, he was hurrying off to talk to him.

With a sigh, Claire waited as her father retrieved another gentleman to introduce her to.

Chapter Two

A half hour later, Nate was no closer to finding a wife than he had been when he arrived at this obnoxious ball. It wasn't that the ladies weren't attractive, but it was nearly impossible to find a suitable match. He should have known that the Season was the perfect grounds for fathers who were so eager to see their daughters marry up that they spent the entire conversation flattering him.

What made matters worse was that Perry had been called away to rescue his ward from another round of drinking with his friends. Had the youth not had a penchant for making poor gambling decisions while drunk, the matter wouldn't be an issue, but as it was, Perry left in haste, leaving Nate without someone to vent his frustrations to.

He scanned the room and saw a gentleman he hadn't spoken to yet. Perhaps this gentleman would steer him in the right direction. Skirting around the area where the couples danced, he reached the gentleman who spoke to Mister Morris.

He waited for the two gentlemen to notice him and offered a slight bow. "Gentlemen."

Mister Morris' grin widened as he and his friend bowed in return. "Lord Roderick, I didn't think you took an interest in the Season."

"My brother's untimely demise a year ago changed that for me," he replied.

"I heard the unfortunate news about your brother," the gentleman standing by Mister Morris said. "He was a good person."

If he had left an heir, he would have been perfect, Nate thought for the thousandth time since he learned of his death. To the gentleman, he offered a smile. "Thank you. I assure you, he's greatly missed. I am Nathaniel Buford, Earl of Roderick."

"It's a pleasure to meet you, my lord. I'm Enoch Morgan, the Duke of Rumsey."

Nate smiled with relief in knowing he was talking to a gentleman who appeared to be of the age where he might have daughters looking to get married—daughters who weren't likely to consider him only for his title since their father was a duke. But to be sure, he asked, "What brings you here tonight?"

"This is my daughter's first Season."

"Really? And where is she?"

The duke pointed in the direction of a young lady dancing the waltz with her partner. Nate tried to determine whether she was interested in the gentleman she was currently dancing with or not. She was smiling and seemed to be talking amiably to him.

"Isn't that Lord Edon she's dancing with?" Nate asked.

Rumsey frowned. "Hopefully not for long. His most notable accomplishments are gambling and women of ill repute. I fear he's taken an interest in her dowry."

Mister Morris chuckled. "I doubt she'll entertain his affections. She's much too smart for that. In fact, if I wasn't already interested in someone, I'd be happy to dance with her."

"I would prefer it if you would," Rumsey told him. "Ideally, my daughter would have a marriage based on more than convenience, but a gentleman who'd treat her well would be best, even if they didn't love each other. A love match might not be common but is ideal."

"You were lucky that way," Mister Morris commented.

Rumsey smiled at whatever memories crossed his mind. "Yes, I was." He glanced at Nate and asked, "Are you looking to get married?"

Taking that as his cue, Nate nodded. "I'm hoping to find a lady whose primary motive isn't marrying up, if you know what I mean."

"You're hoping for a love match?"

He shrugged, unsure if that was the right way to term it. "I'd like someone who can value me for me and not the appeal of my wealth and title."

Rumsey's eyes lit up with appreciation.

"If you'll excuse me, my lords," Mister Morris began, "I think I'll dance."

After they exchanged slight bows, Rumsey shook his head. "You can't blame him for trying, but he'll never win her."

"Win who?" Nate asked, his curiosity piqued.

"I don't know her first name, but her last name is Lowell. He proposed to her last year, but she declined. Between you and me, I believe the reason she declined had to do with his social standing."

"He has no title, you mean?"

"Exactly, though he does have a rather impressive sum of money. Unfortunately, that sum won't buy him a title."

"Poor fool."

"Yes. Poor fool, indeed." Rumsey shrugged. "I tried to explain to him that her father will never agree to the marriage, and she won't run off to Gretna Green so he has no hope of being with her."

"Who is her father?" Nate asked, needing to know which father to avoid in case Rumsey's daughter didn't take a liking to him. He'd already decided he'd pursue her because he liked Rumsey, but he wouldn't force her to marry him.

Rumsey's gaze traveled across the room before he pointed to a round fellow with a jovial laugh who was drinking some wine and talking to a couple of gentlemen. "That's him. Mister Lowell. He saved up a pretty sum of money for his daughters' dowries to attract a suitable husband, but if he thinks money will make his daughters happy, he's sorely mistaken."

"I can't argue with that."

Rumsey turned back to him. "I see the music has stopped. Might I introduce you to my daughter?"

"I would be delighted." As he followed Rumsey to his daughter, who bid farewell to Lord Edon, Nate hoped this would be it. He'd love nothing more than to be done with the blasted search for a wife.

When they reached her, Rumsey motioned to him. "Catherine, this is Lord Roderick."

Nate bowed and she curtsied, and though she wasn't exactly the prettiest lady he'd ever seen, she greeted him in a manner that indicated she'd been brought up to be a proper lady of her future estate. That meant she would ensure her duty in giving him an heir and run the home smoothly. Given that her father was a duke spoke even more in her favor, so he dismissed her homely appearance. Despite what Perry thought, this decision was too important for him to be concerned about a lady's looks.

"I was wondering if I might have this dance?" Nate asked as the music began.

"It would be my pleasure, my lord," she replied in a pleasant tone she most likely employed in all situations.

"I'll leave you two to the waltz," Rumsey said before he left them.

Nate offered his hand to her, and they began the dance. She was light on her feet, proving she was familiar with the dance. "Do you know all the dances?"

"Yes, my lord," she replied.

He couldn't be sure, but he thought she was looking at him the same way she'd been looking at Lord Edon. Not sure how to take that, he cleared his throat and smiled. "Your father tells me this is your first Season."

"Yes, my lord."

"I suppose this must be overwhelming then."

"No, my lord."

He waited for her to continue, but she kept looking at him with the same polite smile that she'd had when she danced with Lord Edon, and it was beginning to make him uneasy. When she didn't explain further, he ventured, "Have you seen the sights in London?"

"Yes, my lord."

Again, he waited, but she didn't volunteer any information nor did she ask him anything. "So what is your favorite sight in London?"

She bit her lower lip as if she was thinking of an appropriate answer before she finally said, "I like them all, my lord."

He sighed. It was apparent Lady Catherine wasn't one for words, but maybe that was a good thing. He could marry her, enjoy a quiet life, and have an heir. Most likely, he'd continue in his political circles while she… While she… He turned his gaze back to her. "What do you enjoy doing?"

She shrugged. "I suppose I enjoy the same things all ladies do, my lord."

"What kind of things would those be?"

"I've been taught to paint, play the piano, sing, dance, be a gracious hostess…"

As she rambled off the list of things she could do, he wondered if any of it truly appealed to her. Her polite smile didn't waver a bit, but he didn't detect the slightest bit of enthusiasm in any of the things she mentioned. He debated whether to ask her anything else, but he figured he already knew how life with her would be. She'd do whatever things proper ladies did with their time. Whether she truly enjoyed those things or not was up to her. As long as she fulfilled her role in running the house, he figured that was all he could expect.

By the end of the waltz, he decided she would do just fine. Sure, she wasn't much of a talker, but really, what gentleman needed the headache of a yapping lady? He needed a lady who would make a good wife, and Lady Catherine met all the requirements. Better yet, she had a father who could be a friend. Life would undoubtedly be easier since he got along with her father. Yes, Lady Catherine would be his wife.

***

"Not that I mind knowing what Napoleon is doing next, but there are so many other things I could be learning instead," Lord Edon said. "Don't you agree?"

Claire kept pace with him during the waltz easy enough, but he talked so fast that she had trouble understanding everything he was saying. One minute, he discussed the weather, the next he was fascinated with the candles in the chandelier, and now he rambled on about how boring political talk was. It didn't help matters that she was beginning to feel overwhelmed with all the new gentlemen she'd been meeting tonight.

She glanced at her sister who was dancing with a viscount, if she remembered the gentleman's title right. Her sister giggled and replied to whatever her dance partner said. Claire sighed. Lilly loved this. The people, the dancing, the merriment… Lilly didn't mind that it was crowded and hot. Lilly didn't feel as if the walls were pressing in on her or that the room was tilting ever so slightly around her.

"Miss Claire?" Lord Edon asked.

She snapped her head in his direction. Since he looked expectantly at her, she decided to agree with him, whatever it was he'd just said. "Yes." She cleared her throat and forced a smile.

"I agree." Hopefully, whatever she was agreeing with was innocent enough.

He nodded. "You're a sensible lady, Miss Claire."

She smiled, hoping to hide her apprehension. Just what made her sensible? She really needed to pay attention to him instead of letting her mind wander.

"Perhaps I should be interested in what the gentlemen in Parliament are doing, but all they do is quarrel. Does God grant kings their authority or is authority chosen by gentlemen? There are better things they could be doing. But no. They argue over things they'll never agree on. Senseless chatter, if you ask me."

Claire thought Lord Edon was engaging in plenty of senseless chatter, too, but kept silent. The thought did occur to her that he might be trying to bore her.

She shook her head. It was none of her business, and she had more pressing things to worry about. Ever since she was little, she didn't do well in large gatherings, and though she managed to cope as she grew older, right now the feeling of being closed in from all sides was getting worse. Mercifully, the dance ended, and by the slight sigh that escaped Lord Edon's lips, she realized he was as relieved as she was.

This was her chance to escape the crowd, even if it was for a few minutes. She curtsied her good-bye to Lord Edon, and before her father could find her in the crowd, she snuck out onto the veranda for a breath of fresh air. She couldn't dance with anyone else, not right now anyway.

For a moment, she leaned against the cool column, thankful for the reprieve. She closed her eyes and took a few deep breaths. As soon as her head stopped spinning, she would be able to go back inside. She kept hoping Lord Clement would return, but so far, he hadn't and she was beginning to give up hope he would. But perhaps he'd pay her family a visit within the next few days. Then if things went well and he fancied her, she wouldn't need to attend another ball, at least not to attract a husband. She had no idea how stressful it'd be to go from one gentleman to another in that room and know each one was sizing her up and trying to decide if she was the right one to give him an heir.

"You shouldn't be out here by yourself."

Opening her eyes, she turned her attention to one of the few gentlemen she hadn't already met tonight. He had coarse dark hair and light blue eyes, broad shoulders that fit his dark clothes rather well, and—her eyes went back up—a surprisingly serious expression on his face. "I can't go back in there right now."

"You can't stay out here unless you have a chaperone. Someone's likely to think you're doing something inappropriate."

Her cheeks warmed. "I assure you I'm not."

"I can see that."

"Then can't someone else see it if they find me out here?"

His eyebrows rose in surprise. "Not all gentlemen who come out here would warn you to go back inside."

"I don't understand what you're implying."

"This is not the best place for an unaccompanied lady to be," he said. "Some gentlemen wouldn't mind enticing you to the gardens."

She glanced at the gardens which was a good distance from them. "I see no reason to go there when it's dark. I wouldn't be able to see anything of interest."

A slight grin crossed his lips before he grew solemn again. "Perhaps not, but I'm sure the gentleman would."

She rolled her eyes and rested her head on the column. The gentleman spoke in riddles, and she had yet to clear her head. "I can't go back inside just yet."

He stepped toward her. "I'm not trying to be rude. I'm trying to protect you from scandal. You are aware of what a scandal is, aren't you?"

She gasped and snapped her head back in his direction, the sudden action causing her surroundings to spin around her. She gripped the column for support. "I'm not an imbecile. Of course, I know what a scandal is, but all I'm doing is resting against a column on the veranda. I'm not far from the ballroom. If someone tries to haul me off to the gardens, I'll dart for the doors."

"You underestimate how quick a gentleman can be."

She narrowed her eyes at him. "Are you such a gentleman? Should I be worried about you?"

He balked. "Good heavens, no. I wouldn't dream of doing anything to tarnish a lady's reputation. Let me escort you back inside, and I'll talk to your chaperone about coming out here with you."

He reached for her but she dodged him. She wavered a bit but held onto the column. "I'll take myself back in when I'm ready." Really! The nerve of him to think she couldn't do such a simple thing herself. All she'd wanted was a few minutes of quiet and fresh air to regroup, and she ended up being harassed.

"You don't look good," he said, concern finding its way into his voice. "You need to go inside."

His insistence that she couldn't take care of herself was irritating her to no end. Just who did he think he was to boss her around? When he reached for her again, she stepped away from him and went to the other side of the column.

"I don't believe this," he muttered and took another step toward her. "You look like you're going to faint. I'm not leaving you out here unsupervised."

She managed to dodge him once more, but in doing so, the world tilted around her and she lost her hold on the column. She let out a scream of surprise as she lost her footing on the edge of the veranda and fell onto the grass. For a moment, she didn't understand what just happened, but then he was kneeling next to her and trying to pull her up.

"I can get up without your help," she insisted, swatting at his hands.

"What is the matter with you?" he asked, partly frustrated and partly baffled.

"Nothing. I just don't want strange gentlemen touching me."

"Strange gentlemen touching you?"

Ignoring the indignant tone in his voice, she rolled on the grass and pulled away from him. As she tried to stand up, the bottom of her dress got tangled around her legs. He placed his hands on her shoulders in an attempt to pull her up. Startled, she tried to push him away and fell back down.

"Stop this indecent behavior at once!" her father shouted.

They stopped and turned their attention to the veranda where a group of people rushed outside to see what caused the commotion. It took Claire a moment to realize how bad the situation looked. Her dress was up to her knees and the gentleman's hands were on her arms. Neither one of them moved for a whole five seconds, and then something snapped and she managed to shove him away. At what was less than a graceful movement, she managed to get to her feet and brushed the lower half of her dress down so she was decent.

"This isn't what it looks like," the gentleman told the crowd. "I was trying to escort her back inside when she tripped and fell onto the grass."

Her sister walked up to their father, a knowing smile on her face. "A likely story."

"It's true," Claire spoke up despite the heat rising up in her cheeks. Truly, she couldn't recall a time when she'd been more humiliated in her life. "I was dizzy."

"Dizzy from lust, no doubt," Lord Edon mumbled, triggering a few giggles from the crowd.

An older lady gave him a sharp look. "I won't tolerate that kind of talk here, Lord Edon."

"My apologies, Lady Cadwalader," Lord Edon replied, sounding appropriately contrite.

Claire's father turned his attention back to Claire and the gentleman standing next to her. "I trust your little tryst will lead to a wedding?"

Claire's eyes grew wide. A wedding? She glanced at the gentleman. It gave her slight comfort to know he was as stunned as she was. Clearing her throat, she ventured, "It was an accident. We weren't…" She struggled to find the right words, but they evaded her.

Lady Cadwalader shook her head. "Don't let Lord Roderick get away with it, Miss."

Get away with it? But there was nothing to get away with!

Lord Roderick sighed, his shoulders slouched.

Lady Cadwalader motioned to everyone to go back inside. "I didn't plan this evening's ball to spend all of my time outside. Lord Roderick, I assume you'll bring her in for a dance?"

Her father nodded to Lady Cadwalader. "I'll make sure he does right by my daughter."

Lord Roderick stiffened for a moment but then offered Claire his arm.

She couldn't believe this was happening. She watched in dread as the onlookers shuffled back inside, either shaking their heads in disapproval or snickering. She mentally cursed herself for taking that last dance with Lord Edon instead of asking her mother to go outside with her so the world would stop closing in around her.

Reluctant, she accepted Lord Roderick's extended arm and walked with him to the veranda. Her father intercepted them and broadly smiled. "Lord Roderick, I'd be negligent if I didn't introduce myself."

"There's no need, Mister Lowell. I know who you are," Lord Roderick muttered as her mother and sister joined them.

"Did my daughter tell you who I was?" her father asked him.

20

Claire felt the tension in Lord Roderick's arm. "Not exactly," Lord Roderick replied, neither smiling nor frowning. "Someone mentioned you by name."

"Oh. Good. At a convenient time, I'd like to discuss your marriage to my daughter."

"Indeed." He shot her a sharp look. "I suppose you'll want an elaborate wedding."

Her jaw dropped. An elaborate wedding? Up to five minutes ago, she wasn't even engaged!

Before she could respond, a cunning smile crossed Lord Roderick's face. "As luck would have it, I need to return to Weston soon. I'm afraid there will be no time for such a wedding. We'll have to make do with a private affair."

She narrowed her eyes at him and removed her hand from his arm. "I don't care. I don't even want to marry you."

"Claire, let's not be rash," her father argued.

"Yes, such a thing would foul up your plans, would it not?" Lord Roderick added.

"I have no idea what you mean by that," she told him, not liking whatever it was he was implying.

"A private affair will be fine, my lord," her father said, shooting her a pleading look to be amiable.

She glanced at her mother and sister who were as happy as her father.

"When do you want the wedding to take place?" her father asked.

Lord Roderick's cold gaze returned to her. "I see no reason to wait. The whole purpose of this marriage is to avoid scandal, is it not?"

She gritted her teeth as her stomach tensed up into a terrible knot. "Is there really no other choice but marriage?"

"Judging by the way you and Lord Roderick were rolling around on the grass together, you must go through with it," her sister said, shooting Claire a congratulatory wink.

21

Claire gasped. "We weren't rolling around on the grass together. I was dizzy and fell."

Her sister shrugged and offered an innocent smile. "From what I saw, you two were intimately entwined."

"That's enough, Lilly," her father admonished. "We don't need to go into details. The important thing is that we'll get the matter resolved and there's no harm done."

"Yes, that seems to be of most importance," Lord Roderick added. "I suppose I should get a special license so we can get the wedding underway. I see no reason to delay the event."

Her father laughed, probably not noticing Lord Roderick's slight grimace. "We'll do everything we can to accommodate you, my lord."

Lord Roderick glanced at her with a clenched jaw. "Splendid."

Claire blinked and then studied her family. Didn't they see how opposed he was to this marriage?

"There's no need to stay out here when we can discuss the details for the wedding inside," Lord Roderick told her father.

Her father nodded and hurried to lead the group back inside, and Claire swore he was half-skipping in his enthusiasm to see her married so well. Without another look in her direction, Lord Roderick followed her father inside with her mother trailing close behind him.

Her steps considerably slower than theirs, Claire trudged after them. Beside her, Lilly whispered, "I never realized you were so clever."

"Clever how?" Claire whispered, clenching her hands together in nervous dread. Good heavens but she was about to be married to a gentleman who detested her because her father made it look like there was a scandal going on when there wasn't!

Lilly giggled but kept her voice low so no one would overhear. "Clever how? The way you plotted to get a gentleman

22

with a title alone with you was genius. I wish I'd thought to go outside by myself so I could snag someone suitable."

She groaned and resisted the urge to rub her forehead as they passed by a group of ladies who giggled from behind their fans. She didn't know what was worse: being stupid enough to go outside without a chaperone or not bolting to go inside as soon as Lord Roderick found her.

"I wonder if something similar might work for me," Lilly whispered.

"Don't be absurd!" Claire quietly hissed. "Do you think he's happy to marry me?" She stopped and motioned to Lord Roderick whose face remained stoic while her father and mother adamantly talked to him.

Lilly shrugged and inspected her gloves. "What does that matter? You'll be wealthy for the rest of your life."

She shouldn't be surprised. Her sister's goal was to marry someone with a title. To her, this was the best thing that could happen to a lady.

"Stop being so glum," Lilly playfully admonished. "Think of all the nice clothes and jewelry you can have. Think of all the servants who'll do your bidding. Think of all the places you can go for entertainment."

She shook her head. Lilly had no idea what she'd just gotten herself into. "He's going to resent me."

Lilly slipped her arm around Claire's and helped her move forward. "Give him an heir and all will be forgiven," she whispered.

She rolled her eyes and ignored her sister's last statement. It was going to take more than an heir to make him understand that she didn't trick him into marriage. What that something was, she didn't know, and truth be told, she didn't even know how to find out.

Chapter Three

Claire gripped the brush in her hands. The previous night had been a disaster. In a week, she was going to be Roderick's wife, and God help her but she couldn't think of a worse fate.

Marion, her maid, entered her small bedroom and offered her a smile. "Would you like me to brush your hair this morning?"

Claire shook her head and absentmindedly ran the brush through it. What did it matter how her hair looked? She'd already found a husband, even if it was due to the manipulations of her family. She never should have left the ballroom without her mother. This was her fault. What she didn't understand was the enthusiasm her father and Lilly had for making it seem as if she'd been in a scandalous situation. Didn't they worry about the family's reputation?

"I think I should brush your hair," Marion told her in a soft voice.

Claire blinked in surprise, not realizing she'd stopped brushing her hair. With a sigh, she handed the brush to Marion and stared off into the distance, not seeing anything in particular. Marion brushed her hair in gentle strokes, something that had a calming effect on her swirling emotions. Claire didn't know how Marion knew what she needed to feel better, but somehow, she did.

Someone gave a tap on her open door. Turning her gaze in the direction of the sound, Claire wasn't sure if she was happy or not to see her sister. For the moment, she greeted her, and Lilly returned the greeting before sitting on her bed to wait in silence while Marion finished fixing her hair. After Marion left the room, Claire faced her sister.

Lilly grinned. "I can't believe your fortune. Imagine snatching an earl so soon!"

Claire groaned. "It won't be a happy marriage."

"Sure, it will. You shouldn't be so glum. I didn't come in to rehash our talk last night. Father wishes to speak to you in the drawing room."

"I'm not sure I want to talk to him right now."

"Oh, do it. Father's not upset."

"*He's* not upset?" Claire snapped but bit her tongue before she said anything else. She stood up and put on her slippers. "Very well. I'll see him."

To her surprise, Lilly followed her out of the room and whispered, "Just think of how big your new house will be. This townhouse is cramped. You'd think Father would rent something better."

"I don't think he could afford to with your new wardrobe."

Lilly shot her a hurt look. "Your wardrobe was expensive, too. Besides, he has money."

"And he's lavished a lot of it on us. To rent a more expensive place would be his undoing." Claire didn't know why she was defending him when he was willing to make her seem like a loose woman to the Ton.

"You're right, of course. You've always been the sensible one of the two of us." She stopped before they reached the stairs and grabbed Claire's arm so Claire paused. She hugged Claire. "I'm happy for you because you're marrying an earl, but I'm going to miss you."

Claire returned her hug. "I'm going to miss you, too."

Pulling away from her, Lilly brushed a tear from her eye. "Please write."

"You know I will, though I suspect you'll soon be married as well."

"I hope so."

"To Mister Morris," Claire clarified.

Though Lilly shook her head, she didn't vocalize her opposition.

Not surprised, Claire went down the staircase and to the drawing room. The door was open, and her father was staring out the window. She was about to ask him what he was watching with such interest, but he turned in her direction and offered her a tentative smile.

"You're not upset with me, are you?" he asked.

"I wish you hadn't done it." There was no sense in pretending she didn't know what he was talking about.

He sighed and motioned for her to sit. When she did, he sat across from her in a chair. "Claire, your mother and I want to see you well off. I've been talking to others to find out which titled gentlemen have good reputations, and Lord Roderick's is ideal. He keeps his financial affairs in order and doesn't engage in frivolous pursuits. When I saw you outside with him, I knew it was the perfect way to secure your future."

"But I wasn't with him the way…the way you made it seem."

"I know. I feel bad about that part. I saw you fall and knew he was trying to help you up." He shrugged. "Your sister went through an entire Season and didn't get married. I didn't want the same thing to happen to you, especially when I could arrange for you to marry someone like Lord Roderick."

"He's not happy about the marriage."

"No. I didn't expect him to be, but he'll have a week to calm down. By the time the wedding takes place, his mood will improve and he'll see you for the wonderful girl you are. Mark my word, he'll be glad he married you."

She didn't agree, but even if she succeeded in convincing her father he was wrong, the Ton was talking about the previous night and would hold it against her. Her only reasonable recourse was to follow through and marry Roderick.

"It will be all right, my dear," her father said in a tender voice. "I wouldn't have done it if I didn't believe that."

She nodded. Even if she didn't agree with what he did, she couldn't fault his motives. He patted her hand and stood up. As he left the room, she closed her eyes and prayed he was right and that in time, Roderick would be glad he had to marry her.

***

Nate knew the exact moment his life came to an end. It was a week later in a small church where he muttered his vows in front of a vicar and the manipulative family who were more than happy about this monstrosity they called a wedding. It was disgusting. Absolutely disgusting. How could he have so easily fallen into their trap?

The wedding was brief, and as he exchanged the vows that sealed his doom, he couldn't help but recall the peaceful life he had envisioned with Lord Rumsey's daughter. So much for that. In one idiotic decision to try to help a naïve lady avoid scandal, he'd plopped himself right in the middle of it and was now paying the price, something that most assuredly pleased Mister Lowell and his daughter to no end.

The wedding was done and over within a matter of minutes, and he waited as patiently as he could for the family to be done hugging each other. At one point, he overheard his deceitful new wife, Blair or something—he didn't pay that much attention when they told him her name—tell her parents that she didn't want to go home with him. He rolled his eyes. If nothing else, he

27

had to admire her ability to play the victim. If he wasn't aware of her father's desire to see his daughters married to titled gentlemen, he would have believed she was innocent.

"You must go home with him," her father softly told her from where they stood several feet from him. "He's your husband now."

She looked over at him, and though he knew he should probably do the decent thing and turn his attention elsewhere, he crossed his arms and stared straight at her, refusing to blink. Did she honestly think it'd please him to be duped?

She turned back to her father and vehemently shook her head and muttered something he couldn't make out, nor did he really care to. If she experienced half the pain he did at being trapped into this horrible marriage, then all the better. If he was going to be miserable, the least she could do was be miserable with him.

After what seemed like eternity, her father and mother managed to push her over to him. "You'll have to forgive our daughter, my lord," her father began. "She's terribly shy."

"Oh?" He glanced at her. "She wasn't terribly shy at the ball when we were outside."

She gasped at his implication, and while something in the back of his mind warned him it was wrong to say that, at the moment, he didn't particularly care to listen to his conscience.

"Come on," he told her, deciding he'd had enough of this stupid game. "Let's go home."

She slapped his hand, but he tightened his grip. She clenched her teeth and stomped her foot on the floor. "No! I demand an annulment."

He laughed. "That's the most absurd thing I've ever heard. You just stood there and promised yourself to me for better or worse." He pointed to the spot where they'd been standing by the vicar whose eyebrows rose. "I'm sorry, my lady, but there's no undoing what God has joined together."

"But-"

"Don't make a scene," her mother warned her daughter in a gentle tone. "You're married now. It's time to act the part."

"Exactly," Nate agreed. "Now come along. I've grown tired of this whole thing."

When she continued to dig her heels into the rug as he attempted to escort her out the door, he picked her up in his arms and carried her out of the church. By the time they were in his carriage, she was crying.

"Your family is no longer around, so you can stop pretending," he muttered under his breath, irritated she continued on in this charade.

"I'm not pretending," she sobbed. "I really don't want to be married to you."

He groaned and handed her his handkerchief. "Do you think you can be done crying by the time we reach my townhouse? I'd rather not have people think the worst, even if I was tricked into this marriage." And how the Ton was already talking about that one! He didn't need them adding, "And Lady Roderick cried all the way home from the wedding," to the gossip. It was bad enough that they agreed to skip the wedding breakfast.

She nodded and wiped her eyes with the clean cloth. "I'll try."

He sighed but kept his thoughts to himself. Anything he'd say would probably make things worse, and as it was, things were bad enough. When she stopped crying, she held the handkerchief out to him, but he grimaced. "Keep it. I have plenty more at home."

Since she didn't say anything, he turned his attention to the horses and carriages as the coachman led them back into the heart of London. Truth be told, he hadn't been opposed to a formal wedding. Indeed, he'd envisioned it when he thought he'd be marrying Rumsey's daughter. But no. Instead, he ended up with a special license, a rushed wedding and a quick departure for home as if he was doing something wrong.

Too bad his friend Perry was back at his estate handling things with his ward. Otherwise, Nate would invite him along and have a couple of drinks to curse money-hungry families.

He let out a long sigh, determined to put all of the horrid events leading up to this marriage behind him. The only thing he could hope for was that she'd give him an heir and then they could spend the rest of their lives ignoring each other. Yes, that would be the new focus. Get the heir and be done with it.

***

Her husband hated her. Claire knew this with all of her heart, and nothing her parents had said would convince her otherwise.

"Give it time. This was sudden. You and Lord Roderick are in shock," her father said.

"He's willing to do the right thing and marry you. He can't be as bad as you say," her mother added.

"But look at the way he's glaring at me," she told them.

None of her protests did any good. They ignored all of her protests, thinking once she got settled into her new life, she'd be laughing about how she imagined Roderick's anger. Except she wasn't imagining it, and no amount of rationalizing it was going to work. Her husband hated her. She had no idea how he felt she'd deceived him into marrying her. She tried to argue for him that he was innocent of any wrongdoing in front of the crowd who didn't believe her. She pleaded for an annulment. She'd done everything she could to let him off the hook, but nothing worked.

Perhaps if he'd taken the time to protest the marriage instead of silently grumbling about it, they could have avoided this whole travesty. But no. He went along with it, and to make matters worse, he implied they were outside doing something they shouldn't be! Why would anyone let her out of the marriage in a situation like that?

The more she thought through everything, the angrier she got. She was outside, not far from the ballroom, and he wouldn't leave her alone. All she needed was a few minutes for the world to stop tilting around her, and then she could return to the ballroom to dance with more gentlemen her father thought suitable for her. A few minutes. Was that really too much for her to ask? It wasn't like she ventured out to the gardens alone. If Roderick had been a true gentleman, he wouldn't have bothered her.

By the time they reached his townhouse, she was no longer trying to hold back her tears. In fact, there were no more tears to shed. At the moment, she was trying to control her simmering rage. As soon as the carriage stopped, she bolted out of it and stormed up the steps to the front door.

"What are you doing?" her husband asked in a mixture of shock and irritation as he stepped out of the carriage.

"What does it look like? I'm going into my new house," she snapped before opening the door.

She ignored the butler and footman and stormed up the first flight of stairs she found. Despite the commotion going on behind her as a confused butler and footman asked Roderick what the problem was, she pressed on. Had she not been so angry, she would never have acted in such an unladylike way. But she figured she had nothing to lose since her husband already loathed her and people were already laughing at her expense.

When she reached the top of the staircase, she pretended she didn't hear Roderick demand she stop. Instead, she proceeded forward, checking each room along the way to determine where her bedchamber would be. She heard his footsteps as he came up the stairs. Startled, she hurried to find the room meant for the lady of the house. To her dismay, he was already closing in on her when she finally found it at the end of the hall.

She glanced back in time to see a scowling earl heading her way. Refusing to let him intimidate her anymore, she scowled in return before darting into the room. It wasn't a lady's room, exactly, but it had a bed, a wardrobe and other items to make her prison comfortable. She tried to close and lock the door before he could reach her, but he stuck his foot in the doorway. She tried to kick it out of the way, but it was no use. He was going to come into the room whether she liked it or not. Groaning under her breath, she left the door, plopped down on the bed, and crossed her arms.

"This is my house," he snapped. "You will not treat my staff that way."

She shrugged as if she couldn't care less what he thought. And really, at the moment, she didn't care what he thought, good or otherwise.

"You have no right to be defiant to me."

She rolled her eyes.

He stood in front of her, his hands on his hips and stared at her.

She refused to look up at him. Maybe if she waited long enough, he'd go away and leave her alone.

"This mess is your doing, Blair, so I suggest you—"

Furious, she made eye contact with him. "Blair? My name isn't Blair." He had just stood there at the wedding, signed the document with her name on it and everything, and he was calling her Blair?

"Whatever your name is, I suggest you—"

She bolted to her feet and glared at him. "My name is not Blair. It's Claire."

"Your name doesn't concern me."

"It should."

"But it doesn't. Your manners, however, are a pressing matter. You don't think the way you stormed into this house and ignored the butler and footman will go unnoticed? People have a tendency to gossip."

"I want you to repeat my name."

He blinked in surprise. "What?"

"My name is Claire. I want you to say it so you'll remember it in the future."

"I won't take orders from you."

She gritted her teeth, her hands balled into fists at her sides. Her husband was impossible. "Doesn't my name matter to you at all?"

"Not really."

"You could at least address me formally since you don't say my name as a term of endearment."

He stared back at her in a silent challenge she was sure was meant to intimidate her into submission.

The insufferable oaf! She had a mind to smack him right upside the head. "I'm your wife. I demand to be addressed with respect."

"That would be true if you had behaved honorably. Since you concocted this scheme to trap me into marrying you, I don't respect you. So no, I won't refer to you as Lady Roderick. But never mind all that. It's done, and until you give me an heir, we'll have to bear with one another."

She cringed at the thought of him touching her. "I can't be with you that way." Especially when he hated her!

"You should have thought about that before your clever little ploy last week. You can't deny me my husbandly rights, so whether you like it or not, we'll be working on getting that heir and we'll start tonight."

Before she could voice her protest, he shot her an amused smile and left her alone.

Chapter Four

$\mathcal{N}$ate slouched in the chair in front of his desk in the library, and though he stared out the window, he didn't see anything. His life kept replaying in his mind. The games he and his older brother had played as children, the realization that titles meant more to ladies than love, the news of his brother's death and funeral. He recalled the ladies his brother fancied but couldn't decide on one he could marry. And it wasn't like his brother was nearing an old age when he fell off his horse and died. At twenty-three, they all thought he had enough time to get a wife and an heir. Nate sighed. And now at twenty-three the responsibility fell to him.

The door to his library opened but he didn't look away from the window. "Lord Clement is here, my lord," his butler called out from the doorway.

Nate motioned for him to let his friend into the room in a half-hearted gesture then let his hand fall limp in his lap. He heard the familiar tap of Perry's cane as he entered the room and managed to turn his head in his friend's direction. Perry limped to the chair on the other side of his desk, so he straightened up and faced his friend. When Perry sat down, he rested the cane against the desk and stared at him, his eyebrows raised in what Nate was sure was amusement.

"I hear you married," Perry said, a slight twitch turning the corner of his lips up.

He scowled. "You missed the wedding by three hours."

34

"It wasn't intentional, Nate."

"I know. It was just as well that you didn't make it. It was more like a funeral anyway."

His friend chuckled. "You shouldn't mope about. Look at the bright side. You don't have to worry about finding a wife anymore. You have her, and now you can have the heir."

"You mean to tell me you haven't heard about my transgression outside Lord and Lady Cadwaladers'?"

"You know I don't pay attention to what the Ton says," he said in a soft voice.

Nate glanced at the cane and knew his friend was right. Why would he pay the busybodies any mind when they pitied him for being born with one leg shorter than the other? It wasn't a big difference, but it did enough to dissuade most ladies from wanting to marry him. "It's unfortunate you wish to marry but can't while I didn't wish for it but had to."

"That's the way it goes sometimes."

Nate stood up and lumbered to a cabinet to retrieve two glasses. After he poured whiskey into them, he handed one to Perry and sat back down. "Are you aware of who my wife is?"

"Yes. I got your missive. You married Miss Claire Lowell."

He gritted his teeth. "Yes. Mister Lowell's daughter."

"I met her."

"Did you?"

"I think she'll make you a good wife. In fact, I came to congratulate you."

Nate grunted. "You are aware that Mister Lowell is ambitious to see his daughters married to titled gentlemen who are wealthy?"

"Yes, I heard of his reputation."

"So what makes you think my marriage to his daughter is going to be a good one?"

"Her father might be ambitious, but he's harmless. He just wants a good life for his daughters. You can't begrudge a gentleman that, Nate."

"Not unless he lets his daughter lure titled gentlemen outside where his daughter figures out a way to create a scandal."

Perry laughed. "That's ridiculous!"

"Is it?"

"Yes. Lady Roderick isn't the type who'd lure you outside."

"Well, she did."

"How?"

"I saw her go out on the veranda so I followed her outside. I suggested she go back in before the wrong kind of gentleman found her and took her into the gardens. She refused to listen to reason and fell onto the grass. I couldn't leave her there, thrashing about like a drunken sailor—"

Perry laughed harder. "Thrashing about like a drunken sailor?"

"You know what I mean."

He shook his head. "I'm afraid I don't. I've never seen a lady fall off a veranda."

"She wasn't exactly graceful as she tried to get up. It's a wonder she managed to walk down the aisle today without tripping on her gown."

"That isn't a nice thing to say," his friend kindly admonished.

"I don't feel like being nice, Perry. The point is, she and her father orchestrated it so that everyone had to come running out to find me trying to help her up. I don't know how she did it, but she made sure her dress was up to her knees. She did a good job of making it look like I was, in fact, trying to take liberties with her. Now I know why she kept pushing me away instead of helping her."

"She was pushing you away?"

"Clever, isn't she? I might detest her, but I'll be the first to admit that she's not stupid."

Perry leaned back in his chair and crossed his legs. "I met her in the ballroom right before I got called away to take care of my ward, and I don't believe she was trying to get you in trouble. I think she's shy. You probably startled her, and when she fell, she was too embarrassed to let you help her."

He rolled his eyes. "You have a lot to learn about ladies."

"One lady who jilted you in the past doesn't make you an expert either."

Granted, his friend had a point, but Nate had accurately assessed the situation and knew what kind of mess he'd gotten himself into.

Perry lifted his glass and held it up. "I propose a toast to you and Lady Roderick. May you have a dozen children together."

Nate growled at him.

Undaunted by his friend's sour response, he drank some whiskey and added, "I know you didn't ask for my advice, but I'm going to give it."

Nate knew this was coming. His friend always found some cheerful way of looking at things, no matter how awful something was and this was no exception. He drank from his glass and reluctantly waited for him to continue.

After taking a sip, Perry said, "You needed to get married, and even though this wasn't what you planned, you should make the best of it."

"That's easy for you to say. You're not the one who had to marry her."

"I wouldn't have opposed marriage with her, Nate, even if the only reason her father would have permitted the marriage was because of my title. She was one of the few ladies who didn't see me with my cane and run away from me."

Startled at the soft tone in his friend's voice, he lowered his glass and studied him. "I'm sorry they do that, Perry."

He shrugged but smiled. "It could've been worse. I could've been born unable to walk."

"True. I don't know how you manage to always look at the bright side, but I admire that about you."

"It's not hard. You just need to think of what you have instead of what you don't. Like you. You have a wife and now can have the heir to secure your family line. I know it's hard to believe, but everything will be all right."

Nate sipped his whiskey and drummed his fingers on the edge of his desk. "Is it going to cause tension because I ended up marrying her when you'd fancied her for yourself?"

"No. Our friendship is too important for that. You both have my blessing."

"Besides her family, I believe you're the only person who is glad for this marriage."

"Once you stop being stubborn, you'll be glad, too, but I can see you won't listen to my words of wisdom anytime soon. You'll need to give the poor thing some grief before you come to your senses and realize what an oaf you're being."

Though Nate scowled, he couldn't be entirely angry at his friend who, once again, had shown how gracious some people could be. "We'll see."

"Yes, we will." He took another sip from his glass and set it on the desk. "I wish I could stay longer, but I need to buy a wedding gift."

"I really wish you wouldn't."

"I have to. You're like a brother to me, and considering all I have are sisters, that means something."

Chuckling, Nate rose to his feet as his friend grabbed his cane and eased out of his chair. "I hope you'll still make it to White's tomorrow."

"You're not going to show your wife around London?"

"I'd rather not spend time with her."

As they walked to the door of the library, his friend asked, "Should I welcome Lady Roderick now or wait until you're in a better mood?"

"She's hiding in her bedchamber. I don't think she'll come down unless someone carries her out of it. As soon as we came home, she ran up the stairs and to the first bedchamber she found that suited her needs."

"You can't blame her for getting away from you. You can be a brute when you're not happy," Perry teased.

"If you continue to take her side, I might refuse to play chess with you in the future."

He let out a gasp. "You wouldn't!"

Nate raised an eyebrow in silent confirmation.

Shaking his head, he led the way out of the room and down the hall. "Send your wife my sympathies."

They stopped at the entrance, and the butler handed Perry his hat.

"Thank you." Perry put his hat on and shot his friend a pointed look. "Be good."

He kept his face void of emotion simply because he knew it would make Perry wonder if he'd heed his advice or not.

Perry sighed before going out the door.

Even though the day hadn't been ideal, Nate realized his friend's visit had cheered him up. Perhaps he'd manage to get through the meal with his wife without scowling at her. That would be a vast improvement over the carriage ride home from their wedding.

Breaking free from his thoughts, he faced the butler. "Is the lady's maid here yet?"

"Yes. She came shortly after you and Lady Roderick arrived."

He blinked in surprise. "She did?"

"I told you. You were in the library."

"Oh." He briefly recalled that the butler had mumbled something about his wife, but he'd dismissed it since he didn't see how the news should apply to him. "Well then, everything is set until dinner." Turning back to his library, he decided to read a book.

***

"You look beautiful, my lady," Marion said as she brushed Claire's hair.

Claire refused to look in the mirror. She didn't want to see everything Marion was doing to make her presentable to that big oaf she was now condemned to spend the rest of her life with. Her gaze unwittingly went to the bed and she shuddered. She knew it was her duty to be with him tonight, but every time she thought about it, she felt sick to her stomach. There was no way she'd be able to eat anything at dinner. As it was, she couldn't even bring herself to drink the water Marion had brought for her.

Marion finished brushing her hair and reached for the pins on the vanity table. "What would you like me to do with your hair?"

"I don't care."

"Then I'll use one of my favorite styles."

Claire glanced at Marion's reflection in the mirror. At most times, she had a tendency to forget Marion was there, but today, she was glad to have her there. Marion was a familiar presence in her new, and very scary, world.

She turned her attention to her hands which were folded on her lap and wondered if she dared to talk about anything personal with her. Up to now, she hadn't. Most of the topics they'd shared had to do with what she might wear or what she might do for the day. Marion had been married, until her husband's death, so she knew about intimate matters.

Marion slipped some pins into her hair. "You'll be happy to know Cook has prepared roast chicken tonight. Apparently, Lord Roderick has good taste."

Claire returned her gaze to Marion's reflection and forced a smile. "I suppose so," she forced out, though she didn't know how she was going eat anything, even if it was one of her favorite meals.

"Lady Claire, in some ways you are like the daughter I never had, and I don't like seeing you this miserable. Is there anything I can do to make things better for you?"

Touched by her concern, Claire made eye contact with her. In all the years she'd known her, Marion hadn't been one to gossip. Perhaps she could trust her in personal matters. Clearing her throat, she managed a weak, "How long does it last?" When Marion's eyebrows furrowed, she pointed to the bed, her cheeks flushed from being so bold.

Understanding lit up her eyes. "Oh! Of course. I should have known that's been troubling you." She offered a kind smile and patted her shoulder affectionately. "I can't say for sure. Some gentlemen last longer than others, but I'd say no more than a couple minutes once he's…involved…in the process. You shouldn't worry so much about it. I know you can't help but feel uncertain about the whole thing, but it's a very natural process and one that brings pleasure." Marion finished pinning her hair back and motioned to the mirror. "What do you think, my lady?"

I think I'm going to throw up, she thought as she glanced one more time at the bed. Swallowing the nervous lump in her throat, she turned her attention to the mirror and studied her reflection. She looked like a virgin all dolled up so she could be sacrificed on an altar.

"You don't seem pleased," Marion softly commented, a worried tone in her voice.

She sighed and turned away from the mirror. "You did a wonderful job. I don't feel up to seeing him, that's all."

"It's just nerves, my lady. Truly, there's nothing to it. All married ladies go through it."

Claire knew Marion meant well, but nothing she could say would ease the sickening knot that tightened in her gut. This just might be the worst night of her life.

Marion smiled and helped her up from the chair. As she adjusted the skirt of her gown, she said, "If you wish to speed things up, be undressed when he comes to you." She stood up and made eye contact with her. "I'll bring up some sherry to help ease your nerves."

"Will that work?"

"Better than you'd think. I use it to calm my nerves once in a while." She walked to the door and opened it.

Claire glanced at the clock on the wall and took a deep breath. This was it. Whether or not she wanted to be in this marriage wasn't up for debate. Now it was a matter of fulfilling her duty and giving her husband an heir.

"My lady?"

Bringing her attention back to her maid, she gave a slight nod of resignation and headed out the door.

Chapter Five

*N*ate hardly tasted his meal. The tension in the dining room was so profound he could hardly stand it. He glanced at Claire who stared at her plate, the food growing colder by the minute. She poked it with her fork before setting the utensil down and placing her hands in her lap. She didn't look at anything but her food. All the fight that'd been in her earlier had departed, and he honestly didn't know if he preferred her when she was arguing with him or completely docile. It was unnerving that a lady could change moods so quickly.

He wondered if he should try to have a conversation with her. He studied her face, noting the furrowed eyebrows and the way she kept biting her lower lip. Steeling his resolve, he decided to keep ignoring her and focused on the rest of his meal. She got herself into this predicament when she trapped him into this marriage. Now she was going to have to deal with the consequences of her actions. Perhaps if she'd carefully thought through the ramifications of what she had planned, she would have sought an earl through honest means.

He dared a look at the servants who waited for him to give the word when he wanted something. "Are you done?" he asked her.

Her head jerked up, her eyes as wide as a scared fox's. He resisted the urge to roll his eyes. She'd been the one to trap him into a hole that he couldn't get out of, not the other way around.

"Before I tell the footman we're done, do you wish to eat anything else?" he clarified, pointing to her plate still full of food.

She shook her head, and he took that as an indication that she was done so he wiped his mouth with the cloth napkin which had been in his lap. After he set it on the table, he nodded to the footman who stood behind his chair and eased to his feet. He waited for his wife to get up, but she remained seated.

Gritting his teeth, he silently counted to ten before asking, "Do you wish to eat something else?"

She refused to make eye contact with him and rubbed her forehead.

Not wishing to involve the servants in their problems, he turned to them. "When—" he closed his eyes for a moment and forced out—"Lady Roderick—" he relaxed—"is done, see to the table." Turning back to her, he managed a slight bow and left the room.

He went to his library and poured himself a drink before he went to his chair and stared out the window. There was no way he could consummate the marriage. Not tonight. Not when things were this miserable. He thought he could go through with it, thinking his sense of duty would strengthen him for the task. But it was no use. He had no desire to force the situation.

Perry told him to make the best of it. Maybe he was right. It wasn't like brooding over the way he'd been trapped was going to change things. Claire was still his wife, and by law, she'd remain as such until one of them died. He just needed to spend enough time with her to get the heir, and God willing, she'd have a boy right away so he wouldn't need to keep going back to her. And maybe in a few days or weeks, they would reach the point where getting started on an heir would be less awkward.

Perhaps this marriage wouldn't be much different from what he envisioned his marriage would've been like had he married the Duke of Rumsey's daughter. Except for the fact that he thought Lady Catherine would be an amiable wife, he didn't get the sense that they'd do much more than show up in public together whenever necessary and ensure he got an heir. The only difference in marrying Claire was that they weren't going to be amiable.

He shrugged and drank more port wine. Well, so be it. This was his lot in life. Having a title meant he had responsibilities. He wasn't promised happiness when he was born.

After an hour passed, he decided he might as well get the ordeal over with. He stood up and headed upstairs, feeling more like a gentleman about to meet his maker than a groom approaching his bride on his wedding night. The door to Claire's bedchamber was shut, which didn't surprise him. She was probably hoping he wouldn't show up, but he couldn't grant her such a reprieve.

As he entered his bedchamber, his valet turned from the nightclothes he set out for him. "Is there anything else you require, my lord?"

"No. This will be it," Nate replied.

His valet adjusted the candles on the dresser before he bowed and left the room, softly shutting the door behind him.

Nate glanced at the door that separated his bedchamber from Claire's and wondered if she had any idea that this particular door existed. Even if she locked the door leading to the hallway, he had a key that he could use in that door. There was no telling if she locked him out, especially after the way she'd been acting at dinner. It would be interesting to find out if she had. Then he'd get an indication of how resistant she was to giving him an heir.

He changed into his nightclothes and tightened the cord on his robe before he left his room, deciding entering through the door adjoining their rooms might frighten her. After thinking over his rehearsed speech for the tenth time, he knocked on the door.

There was no answer from the other side, so he tested the doorknob and was relieved when he realized it wasn't locked. Good. Even if she didn't want him to be there, at least she wasn't going to fight the issue. He didn't relish the idea of forcing his way into her room. The situation was awkward enough as it was. He opened the door. The curtains were drawn closed, but the candles were lit.

Claire was sitting on her bed, gulping down a glass of sherry as if her life depended on it. His gaze went to the almost-empty decanter on the small table next to her. She finished her glass and picked up the decanter to pour the rest of it into the glass, but she missed and some of it spilled onto the rug.

Had he not been in shock at seeing her drink with the abandon of a drunken sailor, he would have acted sooner so he could stop her from drinking directly from the decanter. When she finished, she giggled and set the decanter down with a loud thud on the table. Something in him snapped and he moved forward to grab the glass from her hand before she dropped it.

Holding the glass to his chest, he quickly went to the door and shut it. He didn't think anyone would see them, but there was no sense in letting anyone hear his wife laughing because she was drunk. He returned to her and set the glass on the table. "What are you doing?" he asked his wife as she inspected her gown.

"Did I get any sherry on it?" She hiccupped and giggled. "I love this gown. Lilly hates the color blue. She likes reds and pinks. But I love blue. Blue is so soothing."

He rolled his eyes. What did he care about dress colors?

"I think the gown is dry. I got some on the rug, though."

It took him a moment to realize she was talking about the sherry. She stumbled toward the wash basin, but he stopped her. "Sit down. I'll take care of it."

She crossed her arms and tried to stand up straight but wobbled.

"Here." He led her to a chair and then lit a couple of candles on her dresser so he could see where the sherry was on the rug. "Don't move."

He went to the wash basin and grabbed the clean cloth and soaped it. This wasn't exactly what he thought he'd be doing on his wedding night, but he couldn't have the housekeeper clean the rug and tell the others the lady of the house had to get herself drunk in order to consummate their marriage. He knelt by the rug and washed it clean.

Claire leaned forward in her chair. "Psst."

He stopped scrubbing the rug and looked at her. "What?"

"I spilled some sherry on the rug."

She giggled again as if she thought that was the funniest thing in the world.

With a shake of his head, he returned his attention to the rug and finished cleaning it. He stood up and placed the rag into the basin.

She hiccupped. "I've never had that much sherry before. All I've ever had was a little glass to drink, but this time Marion brought a whole decanter of it."

"So you drank it all?" he asked, surprised she didn't choose to exercise more self-restraint.

With a playful shrug, she said, "I was nervous."

"There's nothing to be nervous about. We're not going to do anything in bed."

She straightened in the chair but swayed to the right before she steadied herself. "We're not?"

Considering she was drunk, he had no idea how well she understood him. "I don't feel like forcing the issue."

She stared at him in a way that made him assume she didn't know what he meant, but then she let out a loud sigh of relief and relaxed in the chair. "Good. I was scared." She giggled and took off her slippers.

"Scared?" What in the world was there to be scared of? By the way she'd manipulated things and then confronted him as soon as they got home, he didn't think anything scared her.

She gave him a surprisingly solemn nod. "Yes." She stood up and carried her slippers to the bed.

She stumbled and almost fell, so he caught her. "Here." Still holding her, he took the slippers and put them at the foot of her bed.

"I've never been with a gentleman before," she whispered and pointed to the bed. "In one of those." She giggled and leaned against him.

"I should hope not."

"I don't know what to expect."

"Well, no one can know until they've done it."

To his surprise, she wrapped her arms around his neck and smiled. "Have you done it?"

"No."

"Are you scared, too?" she whispered.

"No." Good grief. Whatever she found so alarming about the whole thing, he couldn't even begin to imagine. "You have nothing to worry about. I'm going to take you to bed and you're going to sleep. Alone."

"Thank you."

His eyebrows furrowed. "For what?"

"For not making me do this tonight. Marion said the sherry would relax me, but I don't know how good it did. It feels like the world is spinning around me, but I don't think I stopped being scared."

"I don't understand why you'd be scared at all. Annoyed, resistant, begrudging…" Or perhaps she'd feel a mixture of all of those things. "You're scared?"

She snuggled closer to him and lowered her voice. "My mother told me it was painful. She said she cried her first time. Marion said otherwise, but I don't know what it'll be like for me."

He nodded. "I think I understand now." Glancing at her bed, he said, "You need to go to bed. I'll give you something you'll need for that headache you're going to have when you wake up."

She wove her fingers through the hair at the base of his neck. "That is so thoughtful of you. Thank you."

He caught the twinkle in her eyes and the smile on her lips. She was such a beautiful lady. Not only that, but she could be charming when she wanted to be. He cleared his throat. "Yes, well, don't thank me until your hangover passes."

"Lord Roderick," she whispered before he could pull away from her.

"What?"

"Will you kiss me?"

He blinked in surprise. "What?"

"It is our wedding night, and you didn't kiss me at the wedding. Would you kiss me, just once, so I know what it's like?"

"I doubt you'll remember it."

"Please?"

He sighed, thinking this was a bad idea, but he rather liked her this way. She was honest and sweet. Resting his hands on her hips, he nodded. "All right."

She stepped on her tiptoes, closed her eyes, and brought her lips to his. His first instinct was to change his mind because it suddenly occurred to him how personal a kiss was, but then he grew aware of how warm and soft her lips were. He closed his eyes and gave into the pleasure of kissing her. Before he could talk himself out of it, he brought his arms around her and deepened the kiss.

She seemed to melt into him, something he particularly enjoyed. His body responded to her, urging him to continue. He parted his mouth and traced her lower lip with his tongue. She hesitated for a moment but then parted her lips for him, so he brought his tongue into her mouth. It was one of the best things he'd ever experienced, but as much as he wanted to keep going and find out the other pleasures they might share together, he couldn't do it. What he now had with her was a good memory, and he didn't want anything to taint it.

Reluctant, he pulled away from her and turned back her bedcovers. "You need to get your sleep."

Though it was unnecessary, he fluffed her pillow, not sure why he was going through all the trouble except, for the moment at least, he didn't want to dwell on the circumstances that led him into this marriage. It'd been a long and exhausting day. The best thing he could do was let it go for tonight. Tomorrow, he had business to tend to, and he'd be better off if he managed a good night's sleep.

When he turned back to Claire, he saw that she'd taken her gown off. It was on the tip of his tongue to suggest she wait until he left the room before disrobing, but she was slipping out of her undergarments and all he could do was think of how much better she looked without clothes on. He thought to alert her to the fact that he was standing in the room, no less than three feet from her. That might stop her from slowly taking her jewelry off and placing them on the dresser. She was in no hurry to cover herself, and though she couldn't have intended it, it struck him as the most erotic thing he'd ever witnessed.

She then proceeded to remove the pins from her hair, and he didn't know whether to groan in pleasure or frustration. He rubbed his eyes and sighed. She was going to kill him. Slowly but surely, she was going to kill him.

"Isn't it funny?" she asked with a giggle.

Lowering his hand from his eyes, he managed a weak, "Isn't what funny?"

"I'm not nervous anymore." She put the last pin down on the dresser and shook her head so that her hair fell in soft waves around her shoulders. "Maybe the sherry is finally working."

"Finally working?" It seemed to him that it'd been working all along.

"I was still nervous when you came here, but I'm not anymore." She picked up the brush and laughed. "Have you ever noticed how peculiar brushes are? They look like porcupines."

Had she been sober and said that, he would have notified her that she made the strangest observations. But since she was drunk and her breasts jiggled nicely when she laughed, he realized he didn't think it was so strange after all. At this point, he wanted nothing more than to take her to bed and get started on that heir. But it'd be wrong. He couldn't take advantage of her when she was drunk, and it would ruin the nice moment they had when he saw that honest and sweet side of her. That was the lady he wanted to make love to, not the one who had to get drunk to be with him.

He went over to her, gently took the brush from her hand, and set it down. "You need to go to bed. Do you have anything to wear for bed?"

She snuggled against him and giggled. "I don't wear anything at night."

Well, that was all he needed. Now every night he'd know she was in bed naked. With a resigned sigh, he slipped his arm around her waist, trying not to take note of how soft her skin was or the way her curves pressed nicely against him. They reached the bed and he helped her in, parts of her brushing his hands in a way that further aroused him. So much for a good night's sleep.

He pulled the covers up to her chin.

Her eyebrows furrowed. "Aren't you going to come into bed with me?"

"No."

"But I drank the sherry."

"And you'll be hurting tomorrow because of it." He straightened up and blew out the candles. "Sleep well."

Before she could respond, he grabbed the basin, decanter and glass and hurried out of the room so he wouldn't give into the temptation to join her.

Chapter Six

Claire stirred in bed. Her first thought was that it'd all been a horrible dream and that she hadn't married Roderick after all. She thought she'd wake up in her parents' house and laugh the whole thing off, and Lilly would applaud her for aspiring to marry a gentleman with a title. And after they laughed it off, she'd get ready for a ball in hopes of finding a husband.

She opened her eyes and winced at the bright light streaming in through the window. She closed her eyes and rubbed her temples. Then she remembered the previous day. The wedding with a very bitter Roderick, the fight she'd had with him when they arrived at his townhouse, the awkward dinner where neither of them spoke, and then... And then...

Forcing her eyes open, she rolled onto her side where a warm cup of tea was on the table by her bed. She saw Marion come over to her side of the bed and pick up all of her clothes from the floor. She never put her clothes on the floor like that. She made it a habit of putting them in a chair. Rubbing her head, she realized her hair was unkempt. That wasn't right either since she liked to brush her hair and weave it together so it wasn't tangled in the morning.

Everything was off about this morning, and that could only mean one thing: she had been with her husband last night. The problem was, she didn't feel any different. She didn't know if she was supposed to, though. She tried to remember what happened the previous night to get a better idea of what she should be experiencing right now.

She recalled being unable to eat her dinner and leaving for her room, dragging her feet along the way, dreading what was to come. Marion had left the decanter of sherry as she promised. Unsure of how much to drink, she decided Marion knew the right amount she'd need and drank everything in the decanter. From there, things were blurred together. She distinctly recalled Roderick being in the room. Some of the images coming back to her didn't make much sense, like why he'd been wiping something off the rug or why she thought she saw a porcupine when one couldn't have been in the room. But she did remember kissing him and him leading her to the bed.

"How do you feel, my lady?" Marion whispered.

Turning her gaze in the lady maid's direction, she tried to speak but realized her throat was as dry as cotton.

"Here. Let me help." Marion helped her sit up in the bed and handed her the cup of tea. "This will ease the pain in your head. I made it myself with my herbs."

Claire nodded her thanks and sipped it. After another few sips, she realized she could finally speak and said, "I feel awful."

She let out a sympathetic chuckle. "When I came in, the decanter was gone and he left you something for a headache, so I assume your husband took the decanter when he left."

Probably. Claire took another drink, soothed by the warm liquid. "I don't remember anything."

"He must have been in here if the decanter's gone."

"Yes, he was. I remember he was here, but I don't remember—" she shrugged—"being in bed with him."

"Not every lady can say she's had a memorable wedding night. At least it's over and you don't have to worry about the discomfort of the first time anymore."

Yes, that was true. She could now relax and enjoy it as Marion said.

Marion walked over to the wardrobe and opened the door. "What would you like to wear today?"

Thankful Marion kept her voice low so she didn't aggravate her headache, Claire looked at the clothes she'd taken from home. Her father had taken pride in the fact that he could afford the finer dresses, sure that they would suit his daughters when they married. While she had to admit they were lovely, she wondered if it was worth being married to a gentleman who thought she'd tricked him into marriage.

Their strained dinner didn't give her any hope to think she'd ever be anything but someone to give him an heir. She should probably just be grateful he'd been gentle with her last night so she wasn't sore this morning.

Realizing Marion waited for her response, Claire cleared her throat and said, "I'd like the purple dress today."

Marion retrieved it and draped it on a chair by the screen. "Is there anything you'd like to do today, my lady?"

Claire sighed and studied the tea in her cup. "I don't suppose Lord Roderick wants to see me?" Not that she had any idea what she'd say to him if she saw him. It just seemed after they'd been intimate, it was only fitting that they do something together today.

"I saw Lord Roderick leave right before I came up here."

"Oh."

Claire admonished herself for being disappointed. Their wedding had been a disaster, she'd argued with him when they got here, she hadn't said anything to him at dinner, and she had to get drunk to consummate the marriage. What else could she expect?

"Should I get word to your sister that you'd like to spend the day with her?"

Claire looked up from her cup and nodded. "Yes."

"Then I'll do that after you dress for your morning meal."

While Marion finished getting her things ready for the day, Claire drank the rest of the tea, her head feeling a bit better before she got out of bed. Marion helped her dress and decorated her hair with ribbons and pearls.

"I don't see what the fuss is all about," Claire said as she studied her reflection in the mirror. It wasn't like her husband would be there to see her.

"You're a countess now. You should look your best." Marion patted her shoulder. "Besides, you're beautiful. Why hide it?"

Claire smiled at her. "You've always been good to me."

"I think of you as a daughter." She picked up her jewelry and slipped them on her. "How do you feel?" she asked as she clasped the necklace on.

It took Claire a moment to realize Marion meant her head. "Oh, I feel better. There's a slight ache, but it's manageable."

"Good. I'm glad the old remedy worked. Do you feel like eating downstairs or should I bring something up here?"

Claire stood up. "I'll go downstairs."

Marion nodded and turned to leave but then spun on her heel and motioned to the table by her bed. "Lord Roderick left you a note."

Claire waited for Marion to leave before she went to the note and read it. In it, he said he opened an account for her at a clothing store. She glanced at her wardrobe. She couldn't think of anything she needed, except for maybe a nice bonnet.

She put the note down and had breakfast. Afterwards, she went to the drawing room, hoping Lilly could spend the day with her. She didn't see any reason why her sister wouldn't. Since she had nothing else to do, she decided to write about the past few days, pouring her worries and frustrations onto paper so she wouldn't have to keep them bottled up inside.

When she was done, she went upstairs to change into another dress while she waited for her sister to arrive. Once she heard her sister arrive, she hurried downstairs. When she reached the drawing room, she called out to her sister who was staring out the window.

Lilly turned toward her and smiled in excitement. "What a wonderful townhouse! I bet you can't wait to see Lord Roderick's estate."

Claire glanced uneasily at the butler, hoping her husband wouldn't hear about this because if he did, he'd surely be upset. This would only confirm what he thought about her. Hoping to change the topic, she walked over to her sister and asked, "Is there anything you'd like to do today?"

"I wouldn't mind shopping."

Claire had been thinking of doing something scenic, but by the hopeful expression in her sister's eyes, she figured they would do what she wanted. "All right."

Lilly clasped her hands excitedly. "Oh good! I was hoping you'd say yes."

Claire shot the butler another look. The butler wouldn't feel it necessary to talk to her husband about her sister's excitement over shopping, would he? She tried to think of something she might say so it didn't look like her sister came over to spend his money. After a moment of watching Lilly examine the fabric on the curtains, she ventured, "Did Father give you spending money?"

Lilly's eyebrows furrowed. "Did Father give me spending money?" She laughed and shook her head. "Why would he do that?"

Claire sighed in disappointment. No matter how things proceeded from here, it wouldn't look good. Her husband already assumed the worst, and her sister suggesting they shop with her money only supported what he thought. Before Lilly could say anything else to make her look bad, she motioned to the door. "All right, but it must be something small and inexpensive."

"Of course! You don't need to tell me twice."

Unable to make eye contact with the butler, Claire followed her sister out of the room. At the front door, she took the hat the butler handed her, still avoiding eye contact with him. She muttered a weak thank you before slipping out of the house with her sister. The footman opened the carriage door and helped them into it. She informed the footman where her husband had told her to shop. With a nod, he shut the door.

Thankful to get a reprieve from Lord Roderick's townhouse, even if it was for a couple of hours, she collapsed in her seat. She hadn't realized she felt as if she was on pins and needles while in that house.

Lilly wiggled with excitement and clasped her hands together in her lap. "This is wonderful, Claire! That townhouse you live in is gorgeous. There are servants everywhere. And you can buy whatever you want!"

"I can't buy my husband's affections, Lilly."

She waved her hand, dismissing the comment. "Affections won't put food on the table or a roof over your head. You have an ideal setup. Don't worry about things you can't see or touch. Emotions are fleeting. Here one day, gone the next. What you need to do is focus on what'll last. Your husband will pass on his title to your son, and if he dies, you'll still be provided for. Even better, you'll be provided for in style. I hear Lord Roderick manages money very well."

"I'd rather not talk about his money."

"You're right. Why talk about it when you can use it?"

Claire watched as her sister twirled her blonde hair around her fingers. She didn't know what to say to that except, "I hope you don't think I can spend a lot of his money. He opened an account for me, but he told me to be careful with how much I spend."

"You know me better than that. Truly, I don't want much. Just a new pair of gloves and a hat. I also wanted to spend the day with you. You know that, don't you?"

She smiled. "Yes, I know."

"I'm happy for you. You've done so well. I hope by now you're no longer worried about your new role as Lady Roderick."

"Well, no…" She didn't recall being worried about the actual role she needed to play, minus the part that involved giving her husband an heir but it seemed there was nothing to it, at least if sherry was involved.

"Good. Managing a house isn't that difficult. You just need to look good and smile."

Claire thought to remind her sister that there was more to being a wife than what she assumed but knew the words would fall on deaf ears. How many times had she suggested her sister give serious consideration to Mister Morris? Opting to keep her thoughts to herself, she looked out the window as they approached the shops.

Lilly leaned close to Claire and whispered, "So, what was the wedding night like?"

Startled by the change in topic, Claire wasn't sure how to respond.

"I didn't dare ask in the house in case the servants talked, but I've been dying to know what you think. Was it good?"

She studied her sister's wide eyes. She couldn't blame Lilly for being curious, but she had no idea what to tell her.

"Well?"

Claire shrugged. "I don't know."

"You don't know?"

"No, I don't. I drank a lot of sherry last night, and all I remember is that he came to my bedchamber."

Lilly nodded her encouragement for Claire to continue.

"I can't tell you anything else. I was drunk. I vaguely remember kissing him and him taking me to bed. I don't remember anything else."

"Oh." She sighed in disappointment. "That's not very informative."

"I can't tell you anything else. I would if I remembered."

"But you don't remember anything that happened once you were in bed?"

"No."

"Are you sure you two consummated the marriage?"

Claire's cheeks warmed. "Yes!"

"I'm sorry. I didn't mean to upset you."

Lowering her voice, she said, "Forgive me, Lilly. It's hard not to remember something this important."

"There's no need to apologize to me. I should've understood this is a personal matter between you and your husband. I had no right to intrude."

"We're sisters. More than sisters. We're friends."

"Despite our many quarrels as we grew up?"

Chuckling, Claire reached out and held her hand. "The best friends are those you can argue with but love anyway."

"That's true. They see you at your worst and don't run away. If someone can handle you at your worst, they'll stick around for your best." The carriage came to a stop and Lilly glanced out the window. "I hope you'll buy something while we're out. Shopping is more fun when we do it together."

"I was thinking of buying a bonnet. It's a small item."

Lilly giggled and winked. "Jewelry is small."

"No. I'm just getting a bonnet."

With a shake of her head, she said, "You have to start thinking like a countess and enjoy yourself. There's no sense in being frugal."

"I don't need anything else."

"Good heavens, Claire. In your situation, you don't shop because you need something. You shop on a whim. If you see something that you fancy, credit it to your husband's account. Don't limit yourself."

"Only if I want it," she said so her sister would ease up on insisting she buy something she didn't need.

Not that she was actually going to buy more than a bonnet. There was no way she'd take her sister's advice. All she needed was to get into an argument with Roderick because she wasted his money. She followed her sister out of the carriage, praying that the footman and butler didn't make her shopping excursion sound more than it really was.

***

Two hours later, Claire watched as her sister handed the footman another bag of items she'd bought at the store. Her husband was going to kill her. There was no way the footman would be quiet about the amount of clothes and accessories her sister "needed". Claire clutched her stomach, grateful she hadn't eaten much that morning because if she had, she'd be vomiting right about now.

While the footman put the bag next to the others in the carriage, Claire grabbed her sister's hand and led her away from the store entrance so no one mingling about would hear them. "Lilly, you need to return most of those items."

"But I need all of these things." Lilly patted her cheek and grinned. "These things will make me so desirable the titled gentlemen won't be able to resist me. I'm famished. Let's take my things to the townhouse and have a bite to eat before you return home?"

Claire glanced at the stack of boxes and bags in the carriage. Her stomach tightened. There was no way she could eat anything. Not while knowing her husband would most surely confront her about this. Her sister might be enjoying this spending spree, but it was going to give her a heart attack…if Roderick didn't strangle her first.

Lilly wrapped her hand around Claire's arm and pulled her toward the carriage. "Mother and Father would like to see you."

Claire considered her sister's words and decided if she was going to see their parents, she might as well do it today. "All right." She got into the carriage, glad they wouldn't be spending any more money.

Lilly squeezed in next to her and waited for the footman to close the door before she clucked her tongue. "One would swear you married a commoner by the way you're acting. You can't tell me your husband doesn't have the money. Word around the Ton is that he's got more than enough. All the gifts you've so kindly bestowed upon me make him look good. A couple of notable ladies saw what he got me today."

Claire groaned.

With a sigh, she said, "Your husband has more than enough. He's better off than some titled gentleman are. I mean, who would you have married instead of him if given the chance?"

"I thought Lord Clement was nice."

Her sister stared at her for a moment and then laughed. "The one with the limp? Granted, he has a lot of money, but he's hardly suitable for marriage."

"That's a terrible thing to say."

"I'm only voicing what other ladies are saying." Lilly leaned forward and inspected one of her ankle boots. "Do you think we have time to see if a cobbler can fix my sole?"

"I can't believe you, Lilly."

"What? It's starting to come off. You know how dreadful finding a comfortable boot can be, and these are my best pair."

"No, it's not that. It's about Lord Clement. He was very nice, and I believe he'd make a good husband."

"But you're married to Lord Roderick."

Exasperated, she rolled her eyes. "Because I fell and he was helping me up. You and Father came out and told everyone the worst was happening. I had no intention of marrying him." Just how many times did she have to keep saying that?

"Regardless of the circumstances, you are married to him and marriage is permanent. Oh! Unless you plan to be discreet in your affair with Lord Clement once you give Lord Roderick an heir? You can trust me. I won't tell anyone if that's your plan, and it's not a bad one either. Considering Lord Clement's handicap is hereditary, you're smart to avoid passing it on to a child. I just hope you remember to cover his...whatever you call it...with a sheath when you enjoy intimacies."

Claire groaned. "No, I'm not going to take any lovers. I don't want that kind of life." Shooting her sister a critical glance, she asked, "And what is a sheath?"

"It's something a gentleman uses to catch his seed so it doesn't go into a lady's body. That way she doesn't have a child."

Claire gasped, and checked out the window to make sure the carriage was still moving. Turning back to Lilly, she hissed, "How do you know all of this?"

Lilly giggled. "The housekeeper and cook were talking. They didn't know I was listening, but oh my goodness! The things I learned!"

"You're horrible!"

Her eyes grew wide. "Me? Horrible? I wasn't the one talking. I was only listening." She gave a slight shrug. "I was curious. Mother makes it sound like it's nothing more than a wifely duty, so when I heard them talking about how much they enjoyed it immensely, I saw no reason to deny the opportunity to learn why they didn't agree with Mother. Besides, I'd like to know what to expect when my time comes. And now that I know, I won't be so nervous."

"So you already know everything?"

"Well, I can't say they went into a lot of detail, but I put the pieces together."

"Then why did you even ask me about it?"

"To see if your experience was like Mother's or theirs, to find out if it's something you want to do because it's your duty or because you really enjoyed it. You're my sister, and I figure however it was for you will be similar for me. It's a shame you don't remember it. Judging by the housekeeper and cook, it sounds like it's something a lady would want to remember."

"Does it?" Claire asked, not entirely sure that was true but hoping so.

"Yes. They look forward to doing it any chance they got."

"They didn't come out and say that."

"They did."

The carriage came to a stop and Claire sat up straight, adjusted her gloves and took a deep breath. She didn't think the footman would be able to tell that she and her sister were having an inappropriate conversation. At least, she hoped he wouldn't. As long as she gave a polite smile, he would assume they'd been engaging in boring ladies' talk. Oh, how she hoped that would be his assumption!

He opened the carriage door and Claire hesitated but followed her sister out of the carriage. She passed him and swore she saw him snicker at her. But when she studied his expression, his face remained impassive so maybe she imagined it.

She cleared her throat and told him, "After this, I'll be returning home."

"As you wish, my lady," he replied.

It seemed to her that the corner of his mouth curled up into a smile. Her heart stopped. He knew. He just had to know! The shame. He'd tell her husband, and her husband would lose even more respect for her, if such a thing was possible.

"Come on," Lilly said. "I'll faint if I don't eat."

Reluctant, Claire turned from the footman and went over to her sister. With a final glance back at him as he gathered Lilly's packages to bring into the townhouse, she let out a long sigh and headed for the steps. She could only pray that this day wouldn't get worse. But it probably would once her husband found out how much she spent today. Careless spending…the unladylike talk… Too bad she couldn't crawl into a hole and hide there until the next century.

"Claire," her sister whispered.

Turning her attention back to her sister, she joined her and went into the house.

Chapter Seven

"Checkmate," Perry said with a shake of his head as he secured Nate's king. "It's no fun winning when the opponent makes it too easy."

Nate glanced away from the table where Lord Edon was playing cards with some gentlemen. If he didn't know better, he'd swear Lord Edon was trying to lose everything but his shirt. The gentleman had a habit of making outrageous bets.

"Nate."

Nate turned back to Perry and straightened in his chair. "What?"

Perry sat back in his chair and sighed. "Never mind."

Nate motioned to Lord Edon. "Does he make any sense to you?"

"Since when have you tried to figure out Lord Edon?" Perry asked as he set the pieces on the chess board in their proper location.

With a shrug, he watched as Lord Edon made a crude joke that had the gentlemen at his table howling with laughter. He shook his head. How could Lord Edon not care that he could lose so much money?

"You don't usually take an interest in Lord Edon," Perry observed.

Leaning forward so he could lower his voice, he said, "No, I don't, but I've never watched him gamble almost everything away either."

"He likes to live dangerously."

"Carelessly, you mean."

"It's his choice on what he wants to do with his money. Besides, wouldn't you rather talk about Napoleon's move into Germany with a bunch of incompetent recruits?"

Nate shrugged. Talk of the wars didn't interest him at the moment. Today he had other things in mind, more notably the one involving his wife and her comment about being scared to consummate their marriage. Exactly what could possibly scare a lady about something people had been doing since the beginning of time? There was only one person he could think of who'd volunteer the information, and that person was Lord Edon who was, at the moment, referring to the Prince Regent as his hero. Nate resisted the urge to roll his eyes. As if Lord Edon's moral depravity wasn't bad enough.

Perry sighed and grabbed his cane. "I know when I'm not wanted."

Turning back to his friend, he said, "Forgive me, Perry. It's been a long week."

As Perry stood, he gave him a pointed look. "I hope you've been good to your wife."

"You have no need to worry. I wasn't harsh with her."

"Good. I suppose next time I see you, it'll be at Weston."

"Or Blackburn. I don't mind taking the trip to visit you."

"No, Nate. You need to spend time with your wife. Make her happy. Show her that underneath that hard exterior is the gentleman I know who has a heart."

Nate rolled his eyes, purposely facing his friend so he'd see his thoughts on the matter.

"I really should send Lady Roderick a gift to express my condolences."

From Lord Edon's table, the group roared into laughter, and Lord Edon gave a bow as he collected his winnings.

"He's either very lucky or very unlucky," Perry commented. "If you're right and he's trying to lose, he's doing a lousy job of it. However, if he's trying to acquire more, his ability to do so from a gambling table is admirable."

As Lord Edon got up from the table, Nate rose to his feet and pushed his chair in. "Maybe I'll ask him why he's so extravagant with his bets."

"All right."

It occurred to him by the tone in Perry's voice that he didn't believe him, but there was no way he'd even tell Perry that he worried about Claire's fear of the bedroom. Sure, they were friends since childhood, but some things were too personal.

After Perry left the room, Nate made his way over to Lord Edon who drank a shot of whiskey before he turned to leave. "Lord Edon," he called out.

Lord Edon stopped and turned in his direction. "Lord Roderick? To what do I owe this pleasure?"

Glancing around for a private spot, he motioned to a couple of empty chairs by the window. "Do you mind?"

"Of course not."

He followed Lord Edon to the chairs and sat next to him.

Lord Edon picked up the paper sitting on the table between them. "Should I be skimming through the news to have this discussion?"

"No. Why would you think that?"

"Because the wars are all you talk about."

"That's not true."

"It is whenever I hear you speak." With a glimmer in his eye, he chuckled and threw the paper back on the table. "I'm teasing you, Lord Roderick. We both know I don't care about the wars, and you'd have better sense than to ask me about them. So, what desperate thing has brought you to the point where you need to seek me out?"

"I'm not desperate."

His eyebrow rose, and with a disbelieving look, he asked, "No?"

"You're a gentleman of your word when it comes to confidentiality. At least that's what the rumor is."

"It's my only redeeming quality. I've heard enough stories that would make the hairs on the back of your neck stand on end."

"No doubt." Knowing Lord Edon, that had to be true. Making sure no one overheard them, he continued, "What I wish to discuss with you is something you have plenty of experience with."

Lord Edon laughed. "Two compliments in one day. I fear the praise will make me think more of myself than I ought."

"Not praise. Just an observation."

"Now I'm intrigued." Lord Edon leaned forward and looked Nate in the eyes. "You have my word. I'll take what we discuss to my grave. What is it?"

"Well, I…" Despite the heat rising up in Nate's cheeks, he forced out in a whisper, "Is it common for the fairer sex to be frightened their first time…you know?"

Amused, he grinned. "Lord Roderick, you were caught out in the open rolling around on the grass with your wife. Surely, she wasn't afraid of going further."

"I wasn't rolling around on the grass with her. It was a misunderstanding. Do you honestly believe I'd have her right there when I could have taken her to the gardens?"

He shrugged. "I assumed you liked the possibility of being caught."

"Well, I don't. I don't like any kind of scandal."

"That's a shame. I was beginning to respect you. Too bad you're as dull as your reputation indicates."

Nate groaned.

"I'm sorry. We're here to discuss your wife's fear of the bedchamber, correct?"

He nodded.

"Didn't you marry her yesterday?"

"Yes."

"Then that fear should be history. That is, of course, unless you were awful in bed. Is she afraid she'll never climax?"

"No!" A couple of gentlemen looked their way, so Nate lowered his voice and added, "It's nothing like that. I didn't consummate my marriage last night because my wife is afraid to go through with it."

"Really?"

"Haven't you ever had a timid virgin before?"

Lord Edon hesitated for a moment and chuckled. "Sure. I've had all kinds of ladies, whether they were proper or otherwise. It's what I do best, besides gambling and drinking."

"So what do you do to ease a virgin into things?"

"Every lady's different. The best thing you can do is ask her what you can do to make her comfortable."

"Her answer was to get drunk."

His eyes grew wide and he threw his head back and laughed, bringing more unwanted attention their way.

Nate hushed him, and when he finally calmed down, the gentlemen stopped watching them. "I don't want her to be that nervous about it. There's nothing about it that hurts them, is there?"

"I'm amazed. You're an earl, and you have no idea about ladies...at all?"

"I've spent a couple years in political affairs. I'd still be doing that if it weren't for my brother dying without an heir and leaving me with the task."

"Trading boring discussions about laws and wars for a lady's bed? I can see how distressing that is."

He sighed at the sarcasm in Lord Edon's voice. Coming to this rake just might have been a big waste of his time. "I'm not asking for your opinion about my pursuits. I'm asking for your advice on how to make a lady more comfortable in bed. Surely, you know all about that."

"Yes, of course I do. However, you might be better off reading a book on the matter."

"There are books on this subject?"

With an incredulous expression, Lord Edon shook his head. "You poor, poor man. How little you know of the world. There are books on almost every subject imaginable. I have a few such books and more that would make the Archbishop blush. I'll send you one that a mistress wrote. She stated specifically what made her lovers good or bad. You can't get advice better than what you'll get from her, especially with her brutal honesty. I'll send you the book in a package so no one knows what a rake you're becoming in your old age."

He hid his exasperation. Leave it to Lord Edon to enjoy teasing him on such a personal and sensitive matter.

As Lord Edon stood, he added, "I'll be sure to address it from here so no one knows it's from me."

Surprised he chose to be discreet for once, Nate glanced at him as he rose to his feet. "Thank you, Lord Edon."

"I can be a gentleman when the situation calls for it, but let's keep that our little secret. No sense in raising anyone's opinion of me."

Nate wondered what he meant by that but decided it wasn't his business. After thanking him again, he left White's to go to an appointment.

***

When Claire arrived home, she gave a tentative peek out the window as the carriage came to a stop. She couldn't say the day had been a horrible one. She did, after all, get to see her sister and spent as much time as she dared at her parents' townhouse before she felt she'd made the poor footman wait for her too long. Not that he complained. He was very kind during the day, but she still worried he grew weary of her. And now as he opened the carriage door, the looming sense of dread intensified.

"Are you ready, my lady?" the footman asked.

No, she wasn't, but whether she liked it or not, she was home and had to face whatever consequences the day brought with it. When she invited her sister over, she envisioned taking a walk in Hyde Park or seeing a museum. It was supposed to be a relaxing day, one to enjoy before she was whisked out of London and away from her family.

"My lady?" the footman asked.

She broke out of her thoughts and offered an apologetic smile. "I'm sorry." She collected her new bonnet and stepped out of the carriage, glad for his assistance.

"Is there anything else I can do for you?"

"No. I'm fine."

He nodded and closed the door.

She took a deep breath and faced the front door of the townhouse. She could do this. If her husband raised a fuss, she'd tell him her sister was dying and she couldn't deny Lilly her last wish, could she? She grimaced. No. He'd see right through that one. Her sister, after all, was very healthy, and he'd seen her yesterday at the wedding. No. She'd just have to go in there and confront him head on. Squaring her shoulders back, she raised her chin and proceeded up the stairs.

The footman opened the door, and the butler came to welcome her home. As she stepped over the threshold, she asked the butler, "Is Lord Roderick home?"

"No, my lady."

She didn't know whether she was relieved or not. On the one hand, this afforded her a much needed reprieve from the hectic day. A day with her sister, while fun, could also be exhausting, given her sister's fast pace. But on the other hand, this meant it would take that much longer until she and Roderick could have the argument so it'd be done and over with. Considering her options at this point, she decided to retire to her bedchamber and wait for dinner.

She spent an hour at her writing desk, taking comfort in journaling her thoughts. At one point, she glanced around the large room before looking out the window by her desk. Yes, she had everything a lady could want in terms of material possessions.

The townhouse was one of the better ones she'd seen, and she had no doubt Roderick's estate would be even more impressive. The servants were attentive and kind. Marion was a pillar of strength. She could go out and spend the day doing whatever she wanted. For once, she didn't have to discuss her plans with her father and mother. Being married afforded her a new sense of independence she hadn't known before. She'd achieved the aspirations that the other young ladies had hoped for as they entered the Season and married well. So why wasn't she happy?

She stared at the city, noting the hustle and bustle of it all as people went about their business. Not too long ago, she and her sister had been among them. She wondered if anyone else out there was pretending to be happy when they weren't. She'd been pretending. She'd put on a smile and acted as if everything was wonderful, as if being married was the best thing that ever happened to her. But it was expected. Who wanted to pass someone on the street and greet them only to be rewarded with a miserable sigh?

With a shrug, she closed her journal and laid down on her daybed. She pulled the light blanket over her and closed her eyes. The next thing she knew, someone was standing over her, gently calling her name.

She opened her eyes and lifted her head. "Marion?"

Marion smiled. "If you sleep too long, you won't be tired tonight."

"What time is it?"

"Almost four."

She sat up in the daybed and yawned. "Is Lord Roderick home?"

"Not yet."

"Not yet?"

He'd been gone when she woke up and was still not home? Was this how their marriage was going to be? He'd spend all day out, doing who knew what, and then come home for dinner? Then what? He'd stay long enough to perform his duty in getting an heir and then head off again? She frowned. Would he go out again? So the only time she'd see him was at dinnertime and in bed? She just might be sick. Did he dread her that much? And all because he assumed she'd tricked him into marriage?

"Lady Roderick?"

Breaking out of her thoughts, she returned her attention to Marion. "Yes?"

"There are many books in his library, if you're inclined to read."

She nodded and stood. For some reason, this day seemed unusually long. It wasn't even four, and it felt as if she'd been married to Roderick for ten years. God help her manage through a week of this!

Once she reached the library, she scanned the shelves. Her gaze immediately went to the history books. She rolled her eyes. If she wanted to fall asleep again, they would be perfect. She scanned over the other volumes and noticed some were in other languages. Well, there was no way she'd read those. Other books covered topics on wars, politics, the royal line, laws, and other mind-numbing topics. That was it. Tomorrow, her mission would be to find decent books to read. She could see herself dying from many things, but boredom wouldn't be one of them!

The butler came into the room with an object wrapped in brown paper. She walked over to him as he set it on the desk. He jerked when he saw her. "I'm sorry, my lady. I didn't know you were in here."

"What is it?" she asked, motioning to the package.

"A book for Lord Roderick."

"Oh?"

She glanced at the many books lining the shelves. What would Roderick need with more books? If it was something interesting, she could see the point, but as it was, one more boring book wasn't going to make a difference in this place.

"Can I get you anything?" the butler asked her.

She shrugged. "Do you have an interesting book I could read?"

With a slight grin, he said, "I have a few mysteries on hand if that would be to my lady's liking?"

Relieved, she nodded. "Could I read one?"

"I'll retrieve the best one I have."

After he bowed and left the room, she approached the desk and studied the package. She touched it, and sure enough, it was another book, and it came from White's.

"A book arrived for you, my lord," she heard the butler tell Roderick as he entered the library.

She barely had time to turn from the package before Roderick hurried over to pick it up. She wasn't sure, but she thought he looked embarrassed about it.

"I found it," he called out and then darted behind his desk. He slipped it into the top drawer of his desk and looked at her. "Is there a reason you're in here?"

If he hadn't appeared so flustered, she might have been annoyed he decided to hide a book from her, but she found the whole thing amusing. "Actually, I came to find a book to read."

He straightened up and motioned to the books around them. "In that case, have your pick."

"None of them interest me."

"Well, you could buy some. I'll set up an account for you at the bookstore."

She debated whether or not to ask him about the book he just hid but wondered if she knew him well enough to tease him about it. It couldn't be a boring book. Sighing, she decided it might be best to avoid any kind of humor with him. He didn't strike her as someone who knew what a joke was. Clearing her throat, she said, "The butler is lending me one of his mysteries."

He gave a slight grimace before he sat down and gathered some papers to put in front of him. "I suppose they will do for a distraction."

Her eyebrows rose. "What's wrong with a mystery?"

"Nothing. You're free to waste your time as you see fit."

"Waste my time?"

He waved his hand as if to dismiss the irritated tone in her voice. "You're a lady. I wouldn't expect my books to appeal to you."

"By that, you mean that boring books don't appeal to ladies."

He chuckled. "No."

"Then do you mind saying exactly what you mean by it?"

The butler came into the room and handed her his book. "I trust you'll enjoy this, my lady."

She smiled her thanks and waited for him to leave before she turned back to her husband. "He doesn't read boring books like yours," she told Roderick.

"It's not my business what he reads or doesn't read." Roderick scanned a few papers on his desk and set them aside. "I have some things to tend to before dinner. I'll see you then."

She narrowed her eyes at him. "Did you just dismiss me as if I were a servant?"

"No. I—" He looked up at her and sighed. "Well, there is a matter I must discuss with you, and I suppose the sooner I do, the better."

"Oh?" Bracing herself, she got ready for the confrontation she'd been dreading all day.

"Yes." He tapped his fingers on the desk, stood up and went to shut the door.

She took a deep breath. It was so bad he wouldn't let the servants overhear? Well, no problem. She could handle whatever he had to say. In fact, she decided she might as well beat him to it. "Perhaps if you weren't inclined to run off and leave me here all by myself, I wouldn't resort to careless spending."

He paused on his way back to the desk and turned to face her. "What?"

"I will not be guilty of spending money when you are free to run doing who-knows-what all day. Despite your estimation of me, I can understand those books on your shelves, but I have better things to do with my time than to spend it in utter boredom. I choose not to read them, you understand."

"What does this have to do with spending money?"

"A lot, actually. If you'd have thought to take me to the museum or park or some other spot in London, I would have been perfectly happy not to go shopping. Not that I expect you to believe me. You have it set in your head that I only care about money and things it can buy, even when I tell you otherwise."

"Shopping?"

Why should she be surprised that he hadn't heard anything else she just said? Groaning, she said, "Yes. My sister and I went shopping. You can't blame me for it. I didn't want to spend all day here by myself."

"How much did you spend?"

Ignoring the narrowing of his eyes, she told him.

His jaw dropped. "Good heavens! You could have at least been married to me for a month before you spent that kind of money."

"If you had taken the time to be with me or take me somewhere, I wouldn't have gone shopping."

"So I'm to blame for your reckless spending?"

"Well, not exactly. I just can't say no to my sister, and since she's the only one in London besides my parents that I'm comfortable with, I spent the day with her."

"You're not comfortable with me."

"No, I'm not." It was true so why deny it? And why did he act surprised? He must have known!

"So what good would it have done if I had spent the day with you?" He shook his head and turned back to his papers. "Forget it. I have pressing matters to tend to. You spent an outrageous sum of money today. You can't keep running through town as if I'm a prince."

She had a mind to take those blasted papers from him and insist he listen to her—really listen to what she was saying—but what good would it have done? All they would do was go in circles. As long as he believed the worst, all he'd hear were words that confirmed his suspicions. Not knowing what else to do, she stormed out the room.

That night she refused to go to dinner, and she made it a point to lock all the doors to her bedchamber. But he didn't make an attempt to enter her room, and she wasn't sure if she was relieved or upset. After two hours of being in bed, she lit a few candles and started reading the mystery.

Of course, she was relieved he didn't come to her room. It was ridiculous she'd think that just because he came to her room, he'd want to talk to her. The only thing she was good for was getting him an heir, and since he tried for one the night before, there was no point in being around her tonight.

She snapped the book open and gasped. A careful study of the binding assured her she'd done no damage to the book. Good. Not that she couldn't go out and buy another copy for the butler, but the last thing she wanted to do was spend more of Roderick's precious money. She gritted her teeth. She was going to put that thickheaded husband of hers far from her mind and enjoy the murder mystery in her hands…even if it killed her.

Chapter Eight

"*W*e're what?" Claire asked the next morning as Roderick sat across from her at the table.

He grabbed his fork and held it above the baked eggs on his plate. "We're leaving for Weston today."

Stunned, she watched as he started eating his meal. She glanced at her plate full of fruit and eggs and tried to gather up the appetite needed to eat. Sure, she expected to leave London and go to his estate at some point, but she never expected to go so soon after they got married. She thought they might linger on in London until the Season was over. Turning her gaze back to him, she asked, "Why are we leaving today?"

"Because you and your sister don't know the meaning of restraint when it comes to spending money. At least at Weston, my money will be safe."

Her cheeks warmed from a mixture of embarrassment and anger. She struggled with knowing how to respond to him, but so far talking to him had been like talking to a brick wall. The man refused to listen to her so why bother? She placed her hands in her lap and watched him as he continued to eat. She willed him to look up and notice her, but his focus stayed on his plate.

Finally, when she couldn't take it anymore, she took a deep breath, steeled her resolve, and said, "No."

The word, though short and to the point, seemed to echo through the room, and she sensed the servants' surprise. He was, after all, the master of the house and used to being obeyed. But at the moment, she didn't care.

His eyes wide in disbelief, he stopped eating and looked at her. "No?"

"No, I will not go to Weston."

"You can't say no."

"I just did."

"But you're my wife. You have to do what I say."

She shrugged, feigning a bravado she didn't feel. It wasn't like her to raise a fuss. All her life, she'd followed her parents' instruction without a single argument. But something about her husband seemed to bring out the worst in her, and if someone hadn't known her before her marriage to him, they would swear she was one of the most contentious ladies alive.

Grunting, he set down his fork and wiped his mouth with the napkin that'd been in his lap. "It's a pity your father didn't take the time to inform you what your role was to be as my wife before you two conspired to trap me into this farce of a marriage." She opened her mouth to protest that she had nothing to do with it, but he continued, "You are a countess, and I demand you act like it."

Her mouth formed a thin line and she crossed her arms. "You, my lord, are no gentleman, for if you were, you would not talk to me as if I were a wayward child."

"When you stop acting like one, I'll stop treating you like one." He set one hand on the table and stared at her, daring her to respond.

She ran through a list of possible things she might say to put him in his place, but her mind drew a blank. Finally, out of nothing but pure frustration, she snapped, "You have food stuck between your teeth."

Then she threw her napkin on the table and hurried out of the room before he could have the last word. It was horribly childish. She knew this, and yet, she ran up the stairs, nearly tripping on her skirt as she went. When she reached her bedchamber, she collapsed on her daybed in relief. At least for the moment, she was free of the big oaf and his condescending way of looking at her.

Yes, she wished she had been firm and told her sister no yesterday, but she couldn't take it all back and do it differently. What was done was done. And quite frankly, she was in such a sour mood that she'd encourage her sister's extravagant spending today if they went out right now. She closed her eyes and took a deep breath to calm the rage simmering just beneath her surface. It was true. She was a married lady, and it didn't do well to run off like a scared little rabbit in her own home. It probably wasn't a good idea to argue with her husband in front of the servants either. She groaned and rubbed her temples. If only her father hadn't seen it fit to cry scandal at the ball. She might be going to Hyde Park today with Lord Clement. She was sure he would be amiable toward her, unlike Roderick who despised her.

At some point, her anger and lack of sleep from the night before led to exhaustion and she fell asleep. In her dream, she relived that awful night where her fate was sealed with Roderick, and when she stood by him in the small church to repeat her vows, the church melted away and she found herself inside a prison with chains dangling from the stone walls. With a wicked grin, Roderick lurched toward her. She tried to run, but she couldn't move, and before she knew it, he picked her up and chained her to the wall.

She woke with a gasp and jerked up. She rubbed her wrists which felt cold, as if she had truly been in chains. How realistic that dream was!

Marion entered the room with a concerned expression on her face. "Are you all right, my lady?"

Swallowing the lump in her throat, she nodded. "Yes, Marion. I had a nightmare, that's all."

She offered her an understanding smile. "It's jitter, I'm afraid. Once you settle into the marriage, you'll feel better."

Claire doubted it but nodded to appease Marion. Marion went over to the trunk in the corner of the room and opened it.

"What are you doing?" Claire asked, narrowing her eyes as her maid went over to the armoire and opened it.

"I need to pack your things for Weston, my lady," Marion replied.

Claire gritted her teeth. Despite her protests, Roderick was really going to go through with this and haul her off to Weston where she'd be away from her family. She couldn't believe it. Sure, he told her he was going to do it, but a part of her thought he might be bluffing. Well, now she learned he didn't bluff, and even if he intended to go to Weston, that didn't mean she had to. She stood up and debated what she was going to tell that big oaf when she saw him.

"You'll need a suitable dress for travel. Which coach dress would you prefer to wear?" Marion asked, motioning to the blue, maroon, and tan dresses.

With a groan, she picked the blue one. While Marion helped her into it, her mind scrambling for a way she might get out of leaving for Weston. In all seriousness, she couldn't figure out why she needed to go there. It wasn't her who spent the money. But she had a terrible time saying no to her sister, and that was proving to be a disastrous weakness on her part.

"Is there something you require, my lady?" Marion asked, looking expectantly at her.

"Yes. I require a word with my husband. Is he hiding in the library?"

"No. He just left."

Her eyebrows furrowed. "Where did he go?"

She shrugged. "It's not my place to know, my lady, and he didn't say."

She sighed. Maybe it was just as well. It would give her time to figure out what she would tell him when she saw him. "All right. I'll go to the drawing room and send a letter to my family."

They might as well know her new husband was whisking her off to his country estate, making it more difficult to see them. On her way out of the room, she caught sight of the book the butler lent her and retrieved it so she could give it to him. He'd been kind to her in letting her borrow it, and she saw no reason to delay in returning it. She left the room and walked down the stairs. When she reached the bottom, she saw the butler carrying in a new decanter of wine into the library. Curious, she followed him, wondering if her husband was in the townhouse after all. To her surprise, the only person in the library was Lord Clement.

The butler placed the new decanter on the table and looked in her direction. "May I help you, Lady Roderick?"

Lord Clement rose to his feet as she entered the room. Turning her attention to the butler, she held the book out to him. "I wanted to return your book."

He took it. "I hope you enjoyed it."

"I did, thank you. Where is Lord Roderick?"

"Lord Roderick isn't here. He's expected to come back soon."

She nodded, looked at Lord Clement, and decided even if her husband wasn't there, there was no reason why she couldn't make Lord Clement feel welcome. "Are you comfortable waiting in this room? The drawing room seems like a better room to be in until Lord Roderick returns."

"I'll be happy to wait in there," Lord Clement said.

"Would you like tea, my lady?" the butler asked.

"Yes." She motioned for the door. "I'll keep you company, Lord Clement, until my husband returns."

He nodded his consent, so she led the way out of the room and went into the drawing room. She settled onto a settee and waited for Lord Clement to sit in a chair. The butler left so she turned to him and smiled.

"I trust you're doing well?" she asked.

"I manage," he replied, setting his cane by the chair. "I hope my friend isn't being difficult."

Her cheeks warmed. How much did Lord Clement know? Did Roderick tell him she duped him into the marriage? She sighed. Most likely, he had. He and Lord Clement were friends, after all. Around her husband, it was easy to be angry, but under the sympathetic gaze of his friend, she found her wall crumbling.

"It didn't happen the way he thinks," she whispered. "It was an accident. I lost my balance and fell, and he went to help me up." She swallowed the lump in her throat and continued, "He hates me." As soon as she said the last part, she wished she could take it back. Really, she didn't know him well enough to be so intimate in sharing her fears.

The butler came in with the tea and set it on the table.

She waited for him to leave before saying, "Forgive me, my lord. I have no right to say such things to you." She leaned forward and poured the tea into their cups.

"There's nothing to forgive. Lord Roderick and I have been friends since we were children. He's not a hard man to get along with once you get to know him."

"I suspect a friend of his might say that," she mused, thankful he'd been gracious in his reply to her.

"It's true." He accepted the cup she handed to him. "I won't lie, my lady. I would have enjoyed the opportunity to court you, but I believe everything happens for a reason. Lord Roderick is a good man. Stubborn and obnoxious at times, but when it comes down to it, you can trust him to do the right thing. He might not be agreeable now, but he'll come around. Give him time."

"He thinks I trapped him into marriage."

He chuckled. "I heard him explain it. Somehow you managed to force him onto the veranda without a word or a look in his direction."

Her lips curled up into a smile. "It does sound silly when you put it that way."

He took a sip of his tea and added, "An exaggeration on his part. He meant well, of course, when he went to suggest you go back inside."

She couldn't argue that point. "Yes, I suppose he did."

"I know you meant well, too. Sometimes things happen, and you're thrown into a situation you didn't plan on. It'll do him good to have you in his life. He takes things far too seriously. I keep telling him he needs to laugh more."

From what she'd seen of her husband, he didn't smile at all. Even her first impression of him had told her he was unusually serious. But she didn't know what she could possibly do to make him laugh. She drank some of her tea and tried to think of something to say. After a long minute passed, she finally said, "He's decided we're going to Weston today."

"Being away from London will be good for both of you," he replied. "London provides too many distractions. There are too many places to keep you entertained."

"And that's a bad thing?"

"Only if you need to get acquainted with your husband and he needs to get acquainted with you."

"You're right, but I wish I could take my family with me."

He offered her a sympathetic smile. "No one can fault you for that."

Footsteps crossing the hard floors alerted her that her husband had come home. She wasn't sure why she knew it was his footsteps, except there seemed to be a certain hurried pace she'd come to associate with him. He didn't take his time strolling like other people did. Noting the slight trembling of her hands, she quickly set her cup on the tray. The last thing she needed was to spill anything around him because he made it a habit of making her nervous when she wasn't mad at him.

Lord Clement turned his attention to the doorway and called out, "There you are," when her husband entered the room.

Roderick stilled for a moment, glancing from her to Lord Clement.

"I was beginning to think you'd never show up," Lord Clement teased.

She marveled that Lord Clement could be so at ease in Roderick's presence. Her stomach was a bundle of nerves.

"Yes, well, I had to get ready to leave for Weston." He glanced at her again but asked Lord Clement, "How long have you been here?"

"Not long." Lord Clement motioned to the spot next to Claire on the settee. "Why don't you join us? We're enjoying some tea."

"I have something I need to tend to in the library," Roderick said, turning his attention back to his friend.

"You can spare five minutes to drink some tea."

Roderick looked as if he was going to protest but then shrugged and plopped down next to Claire.

"Try not to seem too eager," Lord Clement commented, a twinkle in his eye.

He sighed. "I don't often waste my time sitting in a drawing room when there's work to be done."

Lord Clement's eyebrows rose and he shot her a knowing look.

Despite the awkward situation of being so close to her husband, she chuckled.

As the butler brought in an extra cup, Roderick looked at her. "Do I amuse you?"

"Yes, but for all the wrong reasons," Lord Clement joked.

"You think you're funny." Roderick rolled his eyes as she poured his tea. "It is unfortunate you were born too late to be a court jester."

Claire tried not to laugh again, but she couldn't resist. Roderick's lips turned up at the corners, something that surprised her. She didn't think he ever smiled, even if he could only manage a small one. Apparently, Lord Clement could reach him on a level she couldn't.

Roderick took his cup from the butler, and after the butler left, he said, "I'm sorry I wasn't here when you told me to expect you."

He shrugged. "I didn't mind. It gave me a chance to talk to your wife."

Her husband shifted next to her and glanced at her from the corner of his eye.

"You make a good couple," Lord Clement continued. "I hope you remember that when you're at Weston." Turning his attention to her while Roderick gulped his tea down, he asked, "Has he told you about Weston?"

She shook her head. "No."

"It's beautiful," Lord Clement said. "The land is mostly flat making it ideal for horse riding or taking a walk."

"The manor has vines going up the side of one wall," Roderick added with a grimace.

"The vines give it character. It enhances the manor."

He set his empty cup on the tray. "Enhances how unkempt it is."

Claire noted that her cup was almost full and that Lord Clement was still sipping from his. She couldn't believe Roderick rushed through drinking his tea as fast as he did. When Lord Clement said her husband's mind was on business, he wasn't kidding!

Lord Clement also noticed how quickly Roderick drank his tea, for he asked, "Is this your way of getting me to leave?"

"Leave? You came to me to discuss a matter with your ward. I thought we'd do that in the library." He looked in her direction. "The situation isn't suitable to discuss in a lady's presence."

"No, I'm afraid it's not." Lord Clement finished his tea and set the cup on the tray. "I can take a hint." He rose to his feet and retrieved his cane. "Thank you for a pleasant conversation, my lady." He turned to her and bowed.

She joined Roderick in standing and curtsied. "It was nice seeing you again."

Roderick cleared his throat and told her, "We're leaving in two hours."

She rolled her eyes as the gentlemen left the room, noting that Lord Clement told him he needed to relax more. It really was a shame Lord Clement hadn't been out there on the veranda instead of Roderick. With a resigned sigh, she went to the desk and took out a piece of paper so she could write her family a letter.

Chapter Nine

*N*ate closed the door of the library and faced his friend who settled into the chair across from his desk. "I notice you and my wife are on amiable terms."

Perry snickered as he set his cane against the desk. "And I didn't think you cared about her."

"I was making an observation. It has nothing to do with what I think about her." He crossed the room and poured them some whiskey from the decanter.

"I hope you'll have a gracious disposition when you're at Weston."

As he handed his friend his glass, he shook his head. "I'm taking her there to stop her and her sister from spending all of my money. The two don't know the meaning of restraint. But then, I suppose that's why she married me."

"Oh, Nate. When will you stop fighting her and get to know her? She's actually a sweet lady."

He gritted his teeth and sat across from Perry. He didn't care what his friend thought about Claire. He really didn't. Forcing aside his irritation, he said, "Perhaps if you saw the bill I paid today, you'd be more sympathetic."

"Perhaps you should have set a limit on how much she could spend while she was out shopping?"

Groaning because his friend made a good point, he set his glass on the desk and leaned back in the chair. "I thought you wanted to talk about your ward."

Perry shook his head. "I hope you're being nice to her."

"I don't believe that statement has anything to do with your ward."

"I feel sorry for her. You aren't making this easy for her." Before Nate could order him to get to the point for coming over, he continued, "As for Christopher, I need your advice."

"I thought he was at Harrow."

"He was until he got in trouble. They expelled him."

"His behavior is that bad?"

"I'm afraid so," Perry replied. "His father never showed any restraints, and he's acting just like him."

"Yes, but his father died when he fell off a prostitute's balcony after drinking too much whiskey."

"Do you think logic works on him? The boy is seventeen and reckless. I had to stop him from going out and threatening someone to a duel because Christopher claimed he was cheating at a game they were playing. Thank goodness it stopped with a few punches and broken furniture." Perry ran his hand through his hair. "I don't know what to do. I thought you might have an idea."

Nate leaned back in his chair and considered what he might do with a ward if the young man refused to behave responsibly. After a couple minutes, he said, "Make him a servant. Let him work at the lowest position and pay him, or not, according on the work he does. That should teach him responsibility."

"I have a hard time doing that with my cousin."

"Do you want him to start taking things seriously or not?"

"You're right. All right. I suppose I could make him a stableboy."

"That's perfect," Nate agreed with a smile. "Make sure he gets to clean out all of the horses' stalls."

Despite the grin on his face, Perry admonished, "There's no need to take such delight in forcing him to shovel animal excrement."

"It'll do him good to get an aspect of what he's doing with his life. Even Lord Edon behaves better than him, and Lord Edon leaves a lot to be desired."

"Lord Edon has more sense than to insult a viscount until he's almost staring at the end of a pistol." Perry set his glass on the tray and grabbed his cane. "I hope this works. This time I'll go back to Blackburn with him. So much for finding a bride this Season."

"I'll tell you what. I'll take your ward off your hands and make him a stableboy at Weston. Then you can continue searching for a wife." Nate stood with his friend and placed his glass on the desk. "What a sorry sort we are. You want to find a wife and can't while I don't want one but had one thrust upon me."

"Come now, Nate. You needed a wife."

"Need and want and two different things."

"If it weren't for my limp, I'm sure I could have found one by now."

As they walked toward the door, Nate shook his head. "You could compensate for that by putting something in your shoe."

"Yes but then how would I know she could accept my imperfections?"

With a laugh, he said, "Imperfections or not, you could have a wife. Ladies will overlook a limp if a man comes with a title or money, and you have both. I don't know why you fool yourself into believing you can't get a wife. I'll tell you why you can't find one."

"I was afraid you might."

Hiding his amusement at the sarcastic tone in his friend's voice, he continued, "It's because you spend far too much time chasing your ward."

"You're right. Again. But I'll tell you what *I'm* right about."

Nate stopped at the door and waited for his friend to speak.

"You're afraid there's more to Lady Roderick than spending money."

"I don't know how you deduct that."

"It's easier to keep someone at bay when you think the worst of them, even if the evidence only lies with her parents and sister."

"But if she's part of their family, then don't you agree she'd share their aspirations?"

"Not necessarily. She's nothing like her sister or Hester."

Nate opened the door. "Don't rush on out of here."

Perry jabbed him in the arm. "I look forward to the day where you say I was right."

"You'll be looking forward to it for a very long time because it won't happen."

"This from the same gentleman who was sure his brother would live forever."

"He would have if he hadn't been careless on a horse."

"Give Lady Roderick my condolences."

"Like I said, it's too bad you weren't a court jester."

As Perry left the library, he glanced over his shoulder and added, "Remember to smile."

Grumbling, Nate made sure the butler saw his friend out before he returned to his library.

***

Two hours later while pacing in her bedchamber, Claire made up her mind. Just because she was his wife, it didn't mean she had to go with him. Husbands and wives lived in separate residences all the time. For all she knew, she was carrying his child and her part of the bargain might very well be done. That being the case, she saw no reason to confine herself to his country estate where she'd be without the love and support of her family. God knew her husband wasn't going to give her those things.

Determined, she picked up her valise and opened her door, checking the hallway to make sure no one could see her before she left the room. She debated whether to take the bold approach and walk right out the front door or to sneak off by traveling the servants' stairs. Straightening her back and lifting her chin in the air, she opted for the front door. She was the countess, and that being the case, she had every right to leave in front of everyone.

She strode down the hall and toward the staircase. Her heart raced in anticipation. It wasn't like her to be defiant, but she figured the sooner she stood up for herself and did what she wanted, the better off she'd be in the long run. After all, did she want the big oaf to dictate the rest of her life for her? Today it would be Weston. Tomorrow, it'd be what she could wear and eat. Really, the manipulation had to end somewhere!

A door opened behind her. "Where do you think you're going?" The all-too-familiar stern voice of her husband stopped her in her steps.

With what she hoped was a casual glance over her shoulder so she could judge the distance between them, she said, "I will go where I please."

Then, without waiting for him to head over to her, she ran down the stairs, lifting her skirt and petticoats so she wouldn't trip and fall to her death. Unfortunately, he was too fast for her and blocked her before she reached the final step. She dodged to the side, but, once again, he was too quick for her so she was unable to get around him.

She grunted and stopped trying to bypass him. Looking him square in the eye, she asked, "What do you hope to accomplish by making me miserable?"

"Making you miserable? What about what you've done to me? I was ready to marry the Duke of Rumsey's daughter when you and your manipulative family trapped me into marriage. If anyone's suffering, it's me. And since I have to suffer, you do, too."

She tightened her hold on the valise, wondering why he had to be the one on the veranda that night. Why couldn't it have been someone more reasonable? Probably because someone more reasonable would have left her alone instead of bothering her. "I shouldn't be surprised you'd be this way. You wouldn't leave me alone at the ball, and you won't leave me alone now. If anything, you're the one who trapped us both into this horror of a marriage because you wouldn't leave me alone. So if anyone's to blame for this, it's you." Satisfied, she gave him a firm nod and waited for him to refute that one.

To her disappointment, he was quick to respond. "Ah, but you and your father were waiting for me to go out to the veranda. It was only because I wished to protect your innocence that I followed you. And a lot of good being a gentleman did me."

The footman opened the front door and paused when he saw them. They turned their attention to him, forgetting their argument for a moment. He cleared his throat. "The carriage is ready, my lord and lady."

With a wide smile that implied he enjoyed cornering her, Roderick returned his attention to her and offered her his arm. "Come along. Your carriage awaits."

She frowned at him, not wanting to take his arm but knowing she had no other choice. He'd probably pick her up and haul her to the carriage like he did on their wedding day, and she didn't want to repeat that incident. "Very well, but I won't be staying there."

He laughed in a way that indicated he wasn't the least bit disturbed by her warning.

Gritting her teeth, she marched with him to the carriage. Curse him and his stubbornness! If he would take the time to listen to her—really listen to her, then she might be able to get through that thick skull of his. But no. He made assumptions about her and what was worse, he had a surprising vindictive streak in him. Whatever made her father think Roderick would make a good husband?

She shook her head and glanced at Roderick who watched her with an amused smile on his face. She scowled at him, but this only seemed to delight him more so she quickly turned her attention away from him and let the footman take her valise. With a heavy sigh, she allowed the footman to help her into the carriage and crossed her arms, refusing to look at Roderick as he settled next to her.

"I wouldn't be too depressed, my dear," Roderick said in an annoyingly happy tone. "Soon enough, we'll be at Weston, and you can do whatever you want to. Maybe you'll even discover that you can enjoy yourself without money."

She stared out the window and ignored him.

He didn't say anything else. He simply opened one of his ridiculously boring books and started to read it.

To her surprise, the butler peered into the carriage and held out two books to her. "I thought since you enjoyed the book I lent you, you might find these enjoyable as well."

Touched that he thought to help ease the boredom that was sure to prevail during the long trip, she thanked him and accepted two more mysteries.

Though Roderick's eyebrow rose, he didn't comment.

Good. She didn't care to explain anything to him anyway. The footman closed the carriage door, and she opened the first book so she could start reading, content to forget all about her big oaf of a husband and slip away into another world.

Chapter Ten

*W*hen the carriage pulled to a stop, Claire woke from her slumber. Opening her eyes, she peered out the small window, wondering where they were. Her eyebrows furrowed. "What are we doing at an inn?"

Roderick looked up from the book he'd been reading. "I thought you might like to sleep in a bed tonight. Was I wrong?"

Rolling her eyes, she straightened in the seat, working out the kinks in her back and neck the best she could. Even after all the breaks they'd taken during the very long journey during the day, her body was stiff. "I just didn't realize Weston was so far from London."

"We'll be there tomorrow. In the meantime, we'll make ourselves comfortable here."

She turned her attention back to the window and studied the inn. It looked good enough, but she was surprised an earl would stay at a place that her family could afford. For some reason, she assumed he'd stay somewhere more expensive. Curious, she glanced at him. "Are we suffering financial hardships?"

"That would horrify you, wouldn't it?"

"Forget I asked," she snapped.

He opened his mouth to speak, but the coachman opened the door at that moment. Relieved, she hurried out of the carriage, pretending she didn't notice when she accidentally kicked his foot on her way out. Despite her naps during the trip, she was exhausted. It was only her growling stomach that compelled her to stay awake. There would be time to sleep after dinner.

Roderick got out of the carriage and stood beside her. "Oh good. The roof hasn't caved in yet."

She shot him a pointed look and shook her head. "The inn is in fine condition. I'm not so daft that I can't see that."

Ignoring his nonchalant shrug that almost dared her to doubt her own words, she followed the coachman who picked up her valise and went to the entrance of the inn. If she was smart, she'd ignore Roderick for the rest of their trip. After they went into the inn, she followed the gentlemen up to a room and patiently waited for someone to indicate that she'd be sleeping in a separate room from Roderick's but no one gave her that assurance.

She struggled not to show her apprehension while the coachman brought in the rest of her and Roderick's things. Roderick left the room to talk to the innkeeper, hopefully to get his own room so he'd take his things out of her room as soon as possible. She paced the room, her gaze unwittingly going to the single bed. She tried to focus on other aspects of the room like the beautiful armoire, the large window with simple but pretty curtains, and the oval mirror hanging over a narrow table where a basin and pitcher full of fresh water waited for her to wash up. It wasn't a fancy room by any means, but it was clean and well-kept.

The door to the room opened, so she turned toward it and saw Roderick. She waited for him to shut the door before she spoke. "When will you leave this room?"

"Tomorrow morning when we head out for Weston."

She frowned as he placed his book on a small table by the bed. "Tomorrow morning?"

"Is your hearing all right?"

Her cheeks warmed. "My hearing is just fine. I can't believe you don't have enough money to stay in another room."

"I didn't say I don't have the money."

Taking a deep breath to keep herself from screaming, she pressed as calmly as possible, "Then why are you in my room?"

He sat on the bed and laughed. "Your room? I don't recall anyone saying this is your room."

She crossed her arms. "So do I have a room you'll kindly show me to?"

"Goodness no. This is a popular inn. All the other rooms are full."

"They can't be!"

"I'm afraid they are. We're stuck together in this mediocre room for the night. I hope you can manage it. It's not quite what you believed your life would be like married to a titled gentleman, but it's the reality of it."

She grunted and headed for the door. "I'm going to demand my own room!"

"It won't do you any good."

She paused at the door, her hand on the doorknob. "But you're lying. There are other rooms, and there are probably better rooms."

"We're going to be here tonight whether you like it or not. Even if there are rooms, you don't have the money necessary to pay for it. All the funds are under my control, and that includes your dowry."

Gritting her teeth, she turned to face him. "You're enjoying this, aren't you?"

He shrugged.

She hesitated a long moment, fingernails tapping the doorknob as she tried to figure out the best response she could come up with, but nothing—absolutely nothing—came to mind. She couldn't very well head out of this inn and go back to London right now. For one, he was right here to stop her, and second, she had no way of getting a carriage ride back to London.

Letting go of the doorknob, she made a resigned sigh and went over to the open window. "Since I'm trapped, I suppose I should make the best of it." She glanced at him from the corner of her eye. He settled on the bed and put his hands behind his head, closing his eyes. Irritated, she stuck her head out the window and peered down at the people who were entering the inn. Though she knew it was completely unbecoming of a lady, she let out a shrill laugh. "Oh Lord Roderick, you really shouldn't be doing that, you naughty gentleman you."

To her satisfaction, he bolted up, stormed over to her, and slammed the window shut. "Just what do you think you're doing?"

"Getting my own room, my lord."

"It won't work. Now sit in the chair or on the bed and behave. Dinner will be brought up shortly."

"I want my own room. I know very well you can afford it."

"You're not getting it," he replied, his voice low but sharp.

She glared at him for a long moment, her gaze unwavering from his. She knew full well he was daring her to show a sign of weakness, and she refused to give in. If he wanted to play this game, then she could as well. After a full two minutes passed between them, she straightened her back and lifted her chin in the air.

"Very well," she relented. "We'll share this room tonight." Giving a show of shrugging as if nothing bothered her, she walked by him, intentionally brushing against him so he'd have to step back. "The last time with you wasn't memorable. I see no reason to think tonight will be either."

Even as she said it, she knew she was asking for trouble, but something in her had snapped, and she was too upset to care about propriety. Acting like a lady be damned! The big oaf had it coming!

"Perhaps if you hadn't been as drunk as a lady of ill repute, you would've remembered what happened that night," he shot back.

She clenched her teeth. Blast it! It was just her luck he was quick with a comeback. Tilting her head in his direction, she arched an eyebrow. "And you have experience with such ladies that you would know?"

"I don't believe my affairs are any of your business."

"Neither are mine. Yours." She stopped herself and tried to think of the proper way to word her response. "That is to say that my affairs are not your business either."

He snorted and rolled his eyes. "Not very clever."

She got ready to speak when someone knocked on the door. Closing her mouth, she watched as he crossed the room and opened it. A gentleman brought in a table and a chair. After he set the table down, the other gentleman set a plate full of food down. The first gentleman set the chair in front of the plate. The two gentlemen nodded to Roderick and left.

She furrowed her eyebrows. "So you plan to let me go hungry?"

"I don't know what you take me for," he began, "but I won't let you starve. You'll eat here tonight, and I'll eat downstairs. I won't trouble your pretty little head with the details, but there are ways a gentleman can relax from a long day that don't involve the nuisance of a lady."

"The nuisance of a lady?" She placed her hands on her hips. He had a lot of nerve! "Being around you is as pleasant as having a nail in the foot."

Ignoring what she considered to be a clever retort, he went to the door. "Don't wait up for me. I'll return late."

She gritted her teeth as he shut the door behind him, leaving her alone. She went back to the window and opened it. A quick scan of the area showed her how fruitless it'd be to try to run off, and he knew very well she had no way of getting back to

London. At least not yet. She'd have to wait until they were at Weston. One way or another, she was going to get back to London. Resigned to spending the night in the inn, she turned to the meal on the table and sat down to eat.

***

Nate rolled away from Claire as much as he could in the abnormally small bed. Funny how the bed hadn't seemed so small earlier that day when they arrived at the inn, but in the night when everything was dark, it was definitely small. Perhaps it shrunk.

He gritted his teeth and crossed his arms, willing Lord Edon's book and the memory of Claire as she stood naked in her bedchamber on their wedding night from his mind. Curse them both! He never should have read that very descriptive book on everything a lady enjoyed in bed. It actually included illustrations. And now that he was in extremely close proximity to a lady who felt terribly delightful with curves in so many right places it nearly drove him insane, he didn't know what he was supposed to do.

He debated leaving the bed and sleeping on the floor, but then she'd know she won. And there was no way he was letting her know he was weak! He could insist she act on her wifely duty, but considering the fact that she didn't like him any more than he liked her, lovemaking wouldn't be the pleasant experience he wanted it to be. Granted, he wasn't expecting love and passion, but he had wanted it to be something amiable, something they could both enjoy.

He let out a weary sigh and checked the position of the moon. Just his luck. Dawn was a long ways off. This was, undoubtedly, going to be the longest night of his life. And to think he had ordered the innkeeper to give him one room because he wanted to punish her!

He glanced at her, noting her closed eyes and steady, deep breathing. She was fully clothed—in her morning dress of all things!—tonight, something he supposed he should be grateful for. If he was having trouble sleeping next to her while she wore her clothes, he could only imagine how it would be if she wore nightclothes or nothing. He shook his head in aggravation. Of course, she slept peacefully. She knew it would drive him to distraction to pretend that being so close to him in an intimate place didn't affect her. She was pretending, wasn't she? She couldn't really be asleep. Yes, she was pretending. He was sure of it, and because she was pretending, he couldn't afford to leave the bed.

Determined to see this night through to the bitter end, he rolled over and—not realizing he was already as far at the edge of the bed as he could get—fell to the floor with a loud thud. He bolted up, sure that Claire would open her eyes and prove she hadn't actually been sleeping after all. But to his dismay, she let out a soft sigh and rolled onto her side so that her back was to him.

He rolled his eyes and settled back onto the bed, fully expecting her to give herself away by giggling, but no such evidence of her witnessing his embarrassing fall came. Instead, it was the steady breathing she employed so well. She was either truly asleep or very good at pretending.

Not that it mattered. He'd be better off trying to get whatever sleep he could instead of worrying about what Claire was thinking. Perhaps if he stopped thinking about her and focused on something else, he might drift off to sleep. Willing to give it a try, he took a deep breath, slowly exhaled, and closed his eyes.

Napoleon. He'd think about Napoleon and the battles going on. But that didn't work because when he thought of strategic maneuvers employed in wars, his mind unwittingly went to the strategies outlined in Lord Edon's book—strategies that would ease Claire's discomfort so she might find the consummation of their marriage pleasurable when they finally did it. He gritted his teeth. Fine. So strategies weren't good. Then perhaps he might consider the differing viewpoints from the Whigs and Tories. It seemed to him that his marriage was similar. He and Claire had differing ideas on what a marriage should be like. Granted, there was a factor of convenience inherent for both of them. He needed an heir. She needed security. Of course, she found security in the form of frivolous spending, but could he be surprised? Wasn't that why she went outside at the ball? So she could snare some poor unsuspecting bachelor into a trap?

He opened his eyes and stared at the ceiling. This was ridiculous. He was a grown man. What was he doing by obsessing about something as basic as sex? It was merely a means to get an heir. That was it. Grunting, he sat up, fluffed his pillow and threw it back on the bed before he settled back down. Crossing his arms, he gave up on sleep and stared at the ceiling. There was no doubt about it. While his wife was going to sleep through the entire night, he wasn't. So be it. There was plenty of time to sleep in the carriage, and when they arrived at Weston, the very first thing he'd do was make sure her bedchamber was ready for her so he wouldn't have to share a bed with her for a very long time.

Chapter Eleven

*A*s soon as the carriage pulled up to Weston the next day, Claire breathed a sigh of relief. Now she could finally go back to London! Across from her, Roderick was slumped in his seat, his arms crossed, and his eyes closed. She assumed he was asleep but couldn't be sure.

The carriage came to a stop, and he bolted up in his seat. She jerked in surprise since she hadn't expected his sudden movement. For a moment, they stared at each other, but then the footman opened the door. Neither one of them moved. She furrowed her eyebrows. Why didn't he leave? He hadn't always waited for her to go first.

"Lady Roderick?" the footman asked.

She blinked and turned her attention to him. Clearing her throat, she said, "I am returning to London."

"Oh no, you're not," Roderick argued, his tone leaving no room for argument.

She narrowed her eyes at him. "There's no reason for me to be here."

"There most certainly is. You need to give me an heir."

Shocked that he would dare say that in front of the footman, her cheeks grew warm. "Since you insist on bringing this up right now, I'll inform you that I already did my part. Now it's a matter of waiting, unless you believe yourself inadequate to perform the task the first time."

He gasped. "Might I remind you that such talk is inappropriate in front of others?"

"You're the one who brought it up. Might I remind *you* that if *you* don't want others to overhear what we're saying, *you* need to keep *your* mouth shut until we're alone?" Turning her attention back to the footman, she said, "I demand to go back to London at once."

"She stays here," Roderick ordered.

The footman glanced from one to the other and sighed. "I'll help the coachman with the luggage."

Shooting her a satisfied grin, Roderick left the carriage. She was determined to stay right there in the carriage—forever if she had to—but he grabbed her hand and pulled her into his arms. She wiggled against him in an effort to get away, but he was too strong for her.

"Will you behave or do I have to carry you inside like a wayward ward?" he snapped.

She grunted and pushed against him. "Let me go!"

His hold tightened around her, and he carried her into the house, ignoring the servants who had lined up in front of the manor. Had she not been so upset with him for forcing her to stay here against her will, she would have been horrified that the servants saw everything, but at the moment, she was too angry to think of what they might be gossiping about that night.

He took her to the drawing room and dumped her on the settee. She immediately rose to her feet, but he placed his hands on her shoulders and sat her back down. Before she could make another attempt to bolt for the door, he strode over to the door and slammed it.

Not to be deterred by his anger, she crossed her arms and glared at him. "I will not stay here."

He strode over to her. "We did not consummate the marriage."

She blinked. "Of course, we did. You came to my bedchamber."

"To tell you I couldn't go through with it. I'm a civilized man. I would never force myself on a lady, even if she is conniving."

Her nails dug the sleeves covering her arms. "I've had enough with being insulted. You, my lord, are either deaf or dumb, for nothing I say seems to make little difference. You want to believe I manipulated you into marrying you, then believe it. If you want to believe I wish to run all over London spending your money with reckless abandon, then believe that, too. But don't insult my intelligence by telling me we didn't consummate the marriage." He opened his mouth to speak, but she held her hand up to stop him. She rose to her feet so she could look him straight in the eye. "I could be expecting a child right now, and I can be just as pregnant in London as I can be here."

"I promise you that you aren't with child. Sorry, Claire, but until you give me an heir, you're stuck with me."

"You, my lord, are no gentleman."

"And you, my countess, are no lady." He lifted his chin in the air and looked down at her. "If you refuse to take my word for what did not happen on our wedding night, that's your problem. But I assure you I did not go to bed with you. When your monthly flow comes, you'll discover you are not with child, and at that point, I'll accept your apology."

"Lack of a child won't prove anything. It took my mother a year to conceive my sister."

"At this rate, it'll take us over a year to even consummate the marriage. You aren't leaving Weston until I know you're carrying a child, so if you want to go to London so badly, I suggest you be nice enough to me so we can get the matter over with."

"Be nice to you?" she asked, appalled by his audacity. "When you've done nothing but accuse me of wrongdoing from the moment we were engaged? I suggest you start being nice to me."

"I have been nice to you. In good faith, I let you shop using my credit, and you thought so little of my gesture that you ran amok through the store as if you and that sister of yours had absolutely no clothes."

"I only bought a bonnet."

"You brought her with you." Roderick let out a frustrated sigh and shook his head. "I'm tired of having this argument with you. The fact remains that I am the lord of this estate, and what I say goes. You are staying here until you are with child."

She gritted her teeth as he headed for the door. She closed her eyes and struggled to control the urge to throw something at his head. The big oaf was going to do everything in his power to make her miserable. And all for what? To get even with her for "trapping" him into marriage?

This time when he closed the door behind him, he didn't slam it. Even so, the sound echoed ominously throughout the room. Well, if it was a war he wanted, it was a war he was going to get! She wouldn't be confined to this horrible place just because he wanted it. She'd show him he couldn't control her. Somehow, someway, she would get back to London, and she was going to do it if it was the last thing she did.

***

Two weeks passed, and Claire had no more success in convincing the servants to let her slip out to London than she had the first day she came here. Whatever else could be said for her obnoxious husband, he was a man who commanded unwavering loyalty from his staff. At times, it seemed as if they must think him a god by the way they hastened to do whatever he wanted. And since he wanted her here, they vowed to keep her here as well.

Roderick had taken it upon himself to daily retreat to his library or take a ride on his horse. She didn't miss him. Indeed, she was delighted he left her alone, especially at night. But she was all-too-aware of the absence of a friend, namely her sister. She wrote letter upon letter to Lilly, and Marion arranged for them to be sent out on her behalf. But it did little to ease the aching loneliness that had become her companion.

She did everything she could to fill her days. When she wasn't pleading with one of the servants to take her back to London, she was often in the drawing room using her sketchpad to draw flowers that looked more like warped circles and lopsided ovals than actual flowers. She loved flowers, especially this time of year when they graced the landscape in abundance. She often took her sketchpad with her on her walks along the property, especially to the gazebo, and would sit for an hour trying to improve her sketches of them. Unfortunately, nothing she did worked.

Another week passed, and much to her disappointment, her monthly flow came. She spent a day in her bedchamber, thankful for the tea Marion made to soothe her cramps but also mourning the fact that she wouldn't get Roderick's approval to return to London. She'd have to probably drink more sherry to work up the nerve to have Roderick back in her room. He was still leaving her alone, something she was thankful for, but she knew the reprieve wouldn't last forever. As soon as he found out there was no heir on the way, he'd insist they try again. She could only hope the times when she needed to do her duty were no more than once a month.

Three days after her flow started, she gathered her courage to tell Roderick the bad news. It was before breakfast, before he would run off to ride his horse or read another one of his dull books. She waited for him at the bottom of the stairs, fingering the edge of her yellow dress, her stomach twisting up into knots.

The sound of her husband talking to his valet directed her attention to the top of the stairs. She watched as he instructed the valet on which clothes he'd need after his breakfast. She rolled her eyes. She should have known that on a sunny day such as this he'd be taking a ride on his horse. Sometimes it was irritating to see how much he loved the horse but didn't give her so much as a single thought. She immediately criticized herself for thinking such a thing. What did she care what Roderick thought of her? Just because he was her husband, it didn't mean he was worth her time.

The valet nodded and went to do Roderick's bidding. She sighed and waited for Roderick to stop inspecting himself in the hallway mirror. Finally, he headed down the steps in her direction.

Taking a deep breath, she stood directly in front of him, patiently waiting as he descended each step. It was now or never. She clasped her hands in front of her and watched him. After he went down three steps, it occurred to her that he was going slower and slower with each step. She furrowed her eyebrows.

"Lord Roderick, are you in pain?"

He halted his steps, his gaze meeting hers. "No. Why would you think that?"

"You aren't able to keep up a healthy pace. I simply worried for your health. I could run to London and retrieve a doctor for you, if you so desire."

With a smirk, he twirled around and bounded down the rest of the steps. "There's no need to trouble yourself on my behalf. I've never been better."

"Oh."

"You sound disappointed."

"No, my lord. I assure you I'm quite relieved."

He shook his head but smiled. "You flatter me by your concern. Are you merely inquiring about my health this morning or is there some other, more sinister, deed at work?"

"Something more sinister I'm afraid." She motioned to the drawing room. "It's something better said in private."

His gaze went from her to the drawing room. With a nod, he headed for the drawing room, not bothering to look behind to see if she followed. Not surprised, she went after him and shut the door to the room so they could have some privacy.

She sat on the settee, and she wasn't surprised when he chose to sit in the chair instead of sitting next to her.

"What did you want to discuss?" Roderick asked her as he leaned back in his chair and crossed his legs.

Bracing herself, she said, "I regret to inform you that I am not with child."

He stared at her, not blinking. "And?"

"And?"

"I already told you that you wouldn't be because we didn't consummate the marriage. So what else is there?"

"Nothing. There is nothing else."

She studied his impassive face. He didn't show the slightest bit of surprise over this news. Could it be true that he'd been telling her the truth, that they hadn't shared her bed on their wedding night? She struggled to recall that night, and the only thing that came to her was that he'd been in her room, they'd kissed, and then he was taking her to bed. But had he actually been in the bed with her? She couldn't remember anything else, and for the first time, she considered the reason why she couldn't remember more was because more didn't happen.

A commotion on the other side of the drawing room door interrupted her thoughts. She and Roderick stood, and she hurried after him as he opened the door. In the entryway, the butler stood, listening to an irritated young man who couldn't have been older than seventeen.

"My being here is a mistake," the young man said.

Roderick strode forward and intercepted them. "There's no mistake about it. You are to be our new stableboy, Mister Robinson."

Mister Robinson blanched. "A stableboy? My guardian, who also happens to be my cousin, is an earl."

"Fortunately, I won't let a little thing like you being Lord Clement's ward get in the way of putting you to work." He glanced at the butler. "Kindly escort Mister Robinson to his room." He then turned his gaze to Lord Clement's ward. "You'll find your clothes in there."

"But I brought my own clothes," Mister Robinson argued.

"There's no need. I have everything you need right here," Roderick replied in the controlling manner Claire knew so well. "This isn't a vacation. The sooner you learn responsibility, the better." He gestured to the butler to show Mister Robinson to his room.

The butler hastened to obey, and though Mister Robinson looked like he wanted to protest, in the end, he followed the butler down the hall, his shoulders slumped in defeat. Claire couldn't help but feel sorry for him. In a way, she understood what he had to be thinking. Trapped here, in this house, with someone like Roderick to remind him of everything he'd ever done wrong... She sighed.

Roderick turned to her. "What?"

"Nothing," she quickly replied.

"You think I was harsh on him just now?" he pressed.

Though she didn't wish to get into another argument with him, she figured she might as well answer his question since he asked it. "Very well. Yes. I think you were too harsh. He is an earl's cousin. It seems inappropriate to give him a stableboy's job."

He hesitated for a moment before saying, "If you understood the situation, you wouldn't be in such a hurry to condemn me."

"Then perhaps you'd like to enlighten me?"

"This is a matter between me and Lord Clement, and it's something he wishes to keep confidential."

She considered his words and decided he was right. If Lilly had told her something in confidence, then she'd rather die than tell anyone her sister's secret. She couldn't fault him for doing the same. She indicated her acceptance with a nod and decided she'd eat breakfast while he got things settled with Lord Clement's ward.

Chapter Twelve

*A*fter breakfast, Nate wrote Perry a quick letter to let him know his ward arrived at Weston and had the letter sent to him. He went to his bedchamber where his valet helped him into his riding outfit. The entire time he was getting ready to go to the stable, he wondered if Mister Robinson was giving the stable master any grief. He fully expected him to after all the years Perry had been soft on him. He couldn't blame Perry. Perry had a good heart, but what Mister Robinson needed was the firm hand of discipline.

As he headed out of the house, he caught sight of Claire writing at her desk in the drawing room. He paused for a moment, a slight twinge of guilt nagging him. The weeks at Weston had been long and tense. He didn't delight in keeping her here, despite what she must think. But how was he going to get an heir unless they were under the same roof? If there was another way to do the job, he'd do it. But there was only one way she was going to conceive the heir, and he needed to figure out how in the world he was going to make it happen because as things stood right now, he was going to have to pass on his title to his cousin.

"Are you ready to go riding, my lord?" the butler asked him.

Turning to him, he nodded. "Yes, I'm ready." With another glance at his wife, he saw that she had looked in his direction. Startled, he quickly averted his gaze and strode out the door, not sure why his heartbeat picked up. Clearing his throat, he thanked his footman, who opened the front door for him, and strode out of the house.

He headed for the stable, trying to assure himself he wasn't heartless. Yes, he knew he had avoided Claire as much as he could, but that didn't mean he was insensitive toward her needs. He had, after all, told her the truth: that they hadn't consummated their marriage. Was it his fault if she refused to believe him?

He sighed. If she hadn't gone shopping with her sister, he'd feel safe enough keeping her in London. Why couldn't she exercise more restraint? If she honestly believed she'd consummated the marriage with him, did she assume that potentially giving him an heir meant she could be reckless with his money?

Perhaps if he limited how much she spent at the shops, then they might return to London and she could be happy again? Not that she was happy with him anyway. To her credit, she wasn't putting on a pretense with him. She was letting him know exactly what she did and didn't like. If nothing else, he certainly appreciated that about her.

The familiar guilty sensation returned. Could it be possible she had been telling him the truth—that she had nothing to do with the scandal that led to their marriage? If she had been a part of it, surely, she'd be trying to soften him up in order to get him to allow her greater freedom with his money.

A horse neighed, bringing his attention to the stable. He blinked, surprised he'd already crossed the distance across the lawn. Amazing how a little thing like being preoccupied with guilt should make him forget his surroundings. Taking a deep breath of the warm air cooled occasionally by the breeze, he put Claire far from his mind and focused on why he came out here today.

As he suspected, Mister Robinson was arguing with the stable master. Since the youth's back was turned to him, Nate crept forward, careful that his steps were quiet lest he give himself away. The stable master glanced in his direction once but didn't alert Mister Robinson that he was there.

"I will not degrade myself by cleaning this...this..." Mister Robinson motioned to a stall's floor. After a moment of silence where he waved his hand and shook his head, he finally grunted. "You know the word I'm thinking of here."

The stable master's eyebrows rose. "Manure?"

"Yes. That's it. I will not clean up that filth."

"You are."

"I am not!" He straightened his back and lifted his chin. "I am the cousin of an earl. I have noble blood in my veins. I have people waiting on me. Someday, I will marry a lady of high status, higher than mine, if I dare say so myself, and given where I come from and where I'm headed, I will not touch a shovel that touches that...filth."

Roderick stopped right behind Mister Robinson and clasped his hands behind his back. "You think you're too good to do what Lord Roderick tells you, don't you?"

"You bet I do," Mister Robinson vehemently agreed as he spun around, only to grow pale as soon as he realized who he spoke to.

"You are testing my patience, Mister Robinson," Roderick said, not in the least bit disturbed by the youth's insolence. "I might be a friend of your cousin's, but I will not let that dissuade me from doing what's best for you."

"Best for me?"

"Yes, best for you. You will be an adult soon, and that means you will have responsibilities. I am going to teach you how to be responsible."

"And you're going to start by having me shovel out horse droppings?"

"Yes, and if you can handle the small tasks I give you, you can move on to the bigger ones."

Mister Robinson grimaced.

"If you don't do the work you're assigned in this stable, I will give you a job less favorable."

"I can't imagine anything worse than clearing animal waste."

Nate's lips curled up into a smile. "I can." Before the insolent boy could say anything else, Nate gestured to the stall. "Now go in there and clean it up."

Though Mister Robinson grumbled, he retrieved the shovel from the stable master and went to the stall, tiptoeing his way through pieces of horse manure.

Satisfied, Nate turned to the stable master and waited as he got his horse ready. He watched Mister Robinson who was gingerly digging the shovel under the manure to pick it up. With a grimace on his face, he lifted the shovel and tossed the manure to the aisle of the stable. He shuddered and then turned back to the next piece of manure.

With a chuckle, Nate accepted the reins to his horse when the stable master brought the stallion to him. After he got into the saddle, he left the stable and urged the horse toward the path that would take him past the pond. A ride was just the thing he needed to refresh his mind. Content, he turned his attention to the land around him and enjoyed the morning.

When he returned to the manor, he washed up and changed into new clothes, wondering if he should read a book or attempt to have a conversation with his wife. It was a question he often wondered, and as before, he opted to read a book. He had no idea what he could say to her that she'd find of interest except if he told her she could go to London. Since he had no intention of doing that, he decided it was best to say nothing.

He entered his library and sat at his desk. Closing his eyes, he leaned back in the chair and let his mind wander. The truth was, Claire wasn't the only one who missed London. Parliament was in session, and he loved going to White's to discuss what was happening there, especially with Perry.

The door opened. He sighed and turned his head in the butler's direction, afraid to ask if Claire had, once again, tried to talk him into sneaking her out of the house so she could go to London. Though his servants consistently refused to take her to London, it didn't seem to stop her from asking.

The butler came into the room and handed him a letter. "This came for you, my lord."

Eyebrows furrowed, Nate took it and straightened in his seat. He read it, at first surprised and then worried. Glancing up at the butler who waited for his instructions, he said, "Tell the steward I want to see the ledger."

"Yes, my lord." He bowed and left the library.

Nate read through the missive again. He hadn't had any dealings with Lord Hedwrett. If Lord Hedwrett's letter was to be believed his steward had borrowed money and was trying to pay him back in installments, but Lord Hedwrett wanted all of it back immediately.

He glanced at his books and shook his head. So much for reading. He'd be spending his day working through the budget to find out if his steward was being honest in his bookkeeping. He grimaced. Just what he wanted to do. The steward entered the room with the ledger. Bracing himself for what was most likely to be an unpleasant discussion, Nate motioned for him to sit and got ready to talk to him.

***

That evening before dinner, Claire studied Marion's reflection in the mirror as she was buttoning the back of her gown. "Are you sure there's nothing I can say or do to convince you to take me to London?"

Marion offered her a patient smile. "My lady, you know the answer to that."

"Do you approve of Lord Roderick so much that you'll let me wilt away here?"

"You needn't exaggerate. I've heard stories of gentlemen who are far worse than your husband. Believe me, my lady, he's a good one."

Claire rolled her eyes. This was the same reply she got from all the servants. But still, Marion had been with her for years. Marion ought to understand why she wanted to return to London and see her family. Disappointed, Claire didn't say anything else. She really should stop pleading with the servants to help her get to London. It wasn't doing any good.

Marion finished dressing Claire and patted her shoulder. "Give it time, my lady. You've only been married a short time. Given the circumstances around your marriage, you can't expect things to resolve themselves right away."

Gritting her teeth, Claire forced a smile and left the room. When she reached the bottom of the steps, she was surprised to see that Roderick was getting ready to head out. "Where are you going?" she asked, striding over to him.

As he put on his hat, he turned to her. "I need to verify some financial dealings."

"Are you going to London?"

"No. The business I need to do will be at other gentlemen's estates."

"But can't I go with you?"

Though she suspected a twinge of remorse in his voice, he said, "The business I am tending to isn't suitable for a lady."

She frowned. What, exactly, did he mean by that?

"I won't be gone for long. A week. Two at the most."

"And you're going somewhere that I can't be at?" she asked, her spine stiffening.

"Ladies don't partake of the business I need to tend to," he replied. "I'll return as soon as I can."

She watched as he left, her hands clenching and unclenching. She knew it was her place not to inquire further. What a husband did when away from home was not to be the wife's concern, but even so, she couldn't deny that sting of betrayal she felt in knowing he was most likely running off to a mistress or some unsavory place where prostitutes worked.

"Are you ready to eat, my lady?" the butler asked as he approached her.

Despite her anger, she straightened her back and nodded. If Roderick thought she'd look the other way like other wives did, he had another thing coming. She might not have gotten the marriage she hoped for—one filled with love, but she could find a way to get to London. It was just a matter of looking at her situation from a different point of view. The servants wouldn't oblige her, but that didn't mean all was lost. She could still return to London. And she would. It was just a matter of finding out how she could get around the servants. Satisfied, at least for the moment, she went to dinner.

Chapter Thirteen

Claire let out a weary sigh as she stared out the window of the drawing room. It was cloudy, but at least it wasn't raining. It seemed to her that just about every day since Roderick left, Weston saw rain, as if the whole place mourned his absence. It only added to the gloomy atmosphere around her. At the thought, she rolled her eyes. He'd only been gone for two and a half weeks, but it felt more like months. Perhaps time with his mistress or out gallivanting around with an unsavory crowd amused him enough to forget her altogether.

She struggled not to let his outright rejection affect her, but as the days wore on, she felt herself slipping into a state of limbo—not feeling as if she were truly here and yet knowing she was. The days were beginning to blur into one another, and that morning she had to ask Marion what day it was. Friday. It was Friday. She closed her eyes and repeated it to herself.

"My lady?"

She opened her eyes and turned her attention to the butler who held a missive in his hand.

"This came for you," he said, holding it to her.

Her heart leapt in anticipation as she took it. As she hoped, it was from her sister! "Thank you."

"Would you like me to bring you some tea?"

She nodded and sat on the settee by the window while he left the room. It seemed like years since she'd last seen her sister, and yet, she knew it'd only been a short time. She opened it, eager to find out if her family would make a visit. As she read through the letter, her eyes grew wide. Her sister was entertaining the affections of Lord Hedwrett, and from the way it sounded, her sister was willing to marry him if he proposed.

"Poor Mister Morris," Claire whispered, thinking of the man who'd done everything he could think of to win her sister over.

Claire shouldn't be surprised. Lilly was determined to marry a man with a title, and Lord Hedwrett, a viscount, would do it. With a sigh, she continued reading the letter and noted that her parents would be delighted to come for a visit but wanted to make sure Roderick extended the invitation. Claire placed the letter in her lap and debated when his invite would be possible.

"No! I won't do it anymore. My cousin's an earl. I deserve to be treated better than this!" someone shouted from the hallway.

Surprised, she hurried to the door in time to see an irate young man that she recognized as Lord Clement's ward, shove the butler away from him.

"I have my orders, Mister Robinson," the butler calmly said.

Mister Robinson grunted. "I don't care what Lord Roderick told you to do. I'm not a stableboy. I demand to go home. This place is nothing more than a prison."

She couldn't help but sympathize with him. In many ways, Weston seemed like a prison to her, too. All she did was eat and sleep. Drawing and journaling her thoughts did little to ease the boredom of her life. She closed her eyes and wished she could see her family again. If she could, she'd feel connected with the world again.

The butler glanced her way and bowed. "My lady. May I get something for you?"

Clearing her throat, she shook her head. "No." Ashamed that they caught her eavesdropping, she added, "I think I'll go for a walk."

"Then I need to get you a parasol in case it rains."

Her face grew warm. So she needed something after all. He was right. If she got caught in the rain, she'd need it. As he went to retrieve it, she offered Mister Robinson a tentative smile.

The youth let out a long sigh. "How do you manage it here?"

"I keep busy," she told him, unwilling to tell him the truth.

He stepped toward her and lowered his voice. "I don't know how. I'd die of boredom if it weren't for playing stableboy." He rolled his eyes. "I can't wait until I'm twenty-one. I'm tired of being told what I can or can't do. My guardian is unreasonable."

She didn't know why he was working at the stables, and since it was none of her business, she didn't dare ask him.

"So you had the misfortune of marrying my guardian's friend," he said.

"Misfortune?" She thought that was an odd choice of words. Just what did people say when they talked about her marriage to Roderick?

"I don't know who I feel sorrier for. I mean, I'm forced to clean out stalls all day, and you're stuck inside the house, going about your day doing all the things ladies do." He paused. "What do you do all day in this prison anyway?"

"I write and draw."

"And that fulfills you?"

She shrugged. What was she supposed to say to that? Her purpose wasn't to be fulfilled. It was to give her husband an heir. Outside of that, she didn't know what her purpose was.

Mister Robinson's eyebrows furrowed. "Don't you have any interests besides writing and drawing?"

"I look forward to seeing my family."

He laughed. "That's not the case with me. When I see my guardian coming, I run away from him."

"Lord Clement is a good man."

"People say that, but I have yet to see it, though I will say he knows how to smile, even if it is with fiendish delight."

Despite herself, she chuckled. It wasn't appropriate for her to do so, considering he was mocking Lord Clement. Forcing aside her laughter, she said, "That's not fair, Mister Robinson. You must be respectful of your guardian."

"I know you're right, but I'm rather perplexed my guardian sees it fit to put me under the care of Lord Roderick. And you know what your husband has me doing?"

"Yes, I know."

The butler returned with her parasol, so she thanked him and took it. Since they were watching her, she nodded in their direction and headed for the front door. The butler hurried to open the door for her. Once she was outside, the door closed behind her and Mister Robinson had resumed his litany of complaints.

Though it wasn't raining, she opened her parasol and took a walk along the grounds. She wished she hadn't found Mister Robinson's protests so interesting, but considering how little else there was to do, he had provided the greatest amount of entertainment she'd enjoyed since she'd left London.

She brushed a tear from her eye. How she wished she'd gotten her mother or father to join her on the veranda that night when her fate had been sealed. And now she'd spend the rest of her life in quiet misery, her only reprieve being the times when she could see her family since she had yet to figure out a way to escape.

She passed the flowers that bloomed along the property, but this time, she hardly saw them. She glanced at the front door of the manor and saw Mister Robinson leave for the stables. She stopped walking and watched Mister Robinson as he plopped on his hat and stomped toward the stables. From a distance, it was hard to tell if he was a young gentleman or a young lady. He was wearing men's clothes, of course, but it occurred to her that if she wore similar clothing, she might pass for a stableboy.

As soon as the thought came to her, she rejected it. No. She couldn't do something that outrageous. It was ridiculous she'd even entertain such an idea. She knew the way to London, but she couldn't exactly carry her clothes with her. And she sure couldn't continue on in London dressed in stableboy's clothes.

With a sigh, she turned back to the path and tried to focus on the flowers. They were so pretty. Even with the overcast sky, their colors were vibrant. She supposed she could get her drawing pad and do her best to draw them, even if her talent for it was far from ideal. She went over to the flowers and traced one of the purple petals with her finger. If she could draw it in such a way that it resembled a flower, she might be inspired to paint it and hang it up.

Most of the walls in the manor had nothing of interest hanging on them. Portraits of those who lived there before was about all she'd seen. If she'd known the people, she was sure she'd be interested in them, but in some ways, walking down the hallways and passing those portraits were a bit spooky, especially at night when she imagined those eyes following her. Silly, childish imaginings. She was married now and the lady of a manor. She really should be mature enough to assume her responsibilities, and one of those responsibilities was to stop imagining things that weren't there.

Straightening up, she continued her walk, deciding she wasn't in the mood to draw today. She didn't feel like playing on the piano either, and the servants would have thanked her for that if they'd ever heard her play it. Sadly, she had more talent drawing flowers than she did playing the piano.

Her steps slowed as she approached the gazebo. The sound of a horse neighing caught her attention, so she turned and saw that Mister Robinson was heading her way on a horse. Surprised, she waited for him.

He pulled the reins on the horse when he came within talking distance of her. "You walk almost every day, even when it rains?"

She shrugged. "I like to walk."

"There's no denying that, but I can't help but notice you aren't smiling."

She didn't know what to say to that so she kept silent. She glanced at the gazebo where she usually sat for a while during the day and let her mind wander. With him staring at her, she thought it'd be rude to do so now, but at the same time, she had no idea what to say to him.

"Lady Roderick, isn't there something you want to do? Something that will bring a smile to your face?"

She turned her attention back to him, wondering if she should be reading more into his suggestive smile than she initially had. "Where are you going with this?"

"I thought perhaps you might like to try something new."

She narrowed her eyes at him. "New in what way?"

He laughed and shook his head. "Pardon me, my lady. I meant nothing inappropriate, I assure you. I only meant to ask if there's anything I can do to help ease the burden of living in this dreadful place? I was wondering if I can do something to bring some light to your dark world."

"The only thing that would brighten my day is if I saw my family, especially my sister."

"Your sister?"

"Yes, she and I are close. That is, we were close. But then I married, and..." Unable to find the words to continue, she shrugged.

"I understand." He sat back in the saddle and slapped his hand on his leg. "You need to visit your family. That's easy enough. Tell the footman and coach driver to take you to her residence."

"I can't," she slowly replied.

"Do you need an invitation?"

"No. They won't take me there without Lord Roderick's approval."

Mister Robinson grunted and rolled his eyes. "Not without Lord Roderick's approval? You're his wife, not his ward."

"But he is my husband, and they listen to him before they listen to me."

"Well, he's not here now. And when he was here, he kept to himself to the point where I began to wonder if I imagined him."

"No, you didn't imagine him. He's very real." Though she knew it was wrong, she quickly added, "I've seen him scowl with grave disapproval many times, so I know this for a fact."

His eyes lit up and he chuckled. "You have a marvelous sense of humor, my lady. One wouldn't think it upon first meeting you. I suspect the almighty Lord Roderick's scowls have had an unpleasant effect on you."

"There are certain things about our marriage that—" She stopped herself in time before she embarrassed herself. Mister Robinson was cunning in extracting information from her, but she'd told him more than enough already and was determined that she wouldn't say any more.

He shrugged. "Some gentlemen are unlovable. It can't be helped." He studied the sky for a moment and then grinned. "You should see your family. How far are they from here?"

"I'm afraid it'd take two days to get there. I can't leave in the morning and come back in the evening."

"So? You don't need anyone's permission to go. Stay there for a few days. Even better than that, stay there forever. Then you can get out of this prison. I know I'd never come back if it was me."

She shook her head. "I can't run out of here with the carriage. It's so big everyone will notice me. And I can't travel alone on horseback because I'm not a gentleman."

His lips curled up into a wide smile. "Lady Roderick, you have a terrific idea!"

"No. I can't do it."

"Of course you can."

She shook her head. No, she couldn't. There was no way she could.

"You don't have to be a gentleman to look like one. I could lend you my stableboy's clothes."

"But I couldn't keep stableboy clothes while in London."

"I'm sure your family can provide ladies' clothes upon your arrival. If you want to get out of here, then do it."

She was ready to argue, but the more she considered his words, the more she realized he was right. She could do it. She could get out of this place. This was the break she needed! No one else was willing to help her, but Mister Robinson was. With a firm nod, she said, "All right. I'll do it."

Mister Robinson laughed. "Marvelous, Lady Roderick. It'll be our secret. I won't tell a soul. I'll set out a pair of clothes for you on the small shelf behind the servants' stairs. Do you know where that is?"

"Yes."

"Good. Get them late tonight when everyone's asleep. Then after breakfast, come to the stable dressed up as a stableboy. I'll help gather enough food and water for your trip and find you a suitable horse so you can be on your way."

She nodded her agreement and watched as he rode back to the stable. It was a gamble. This could backfire on her, but she was desperate to try anything at this point. And though Mister Robinson was known for getting in trouble, she sensed that deep down, he was someone she could trust.

Taking a deep breath to calm her racing heart, she turned toward the gazebo but realized she didn't want to sit there today. No. Today she wanted to think upon this new plan to get away from Weston, and if Roderick came after her, she'd deal with the consequences then.

***

That night while in the carriage on his way back to Weston, Nate couldn't seem to push aside the nagging feeling that he'd somehow pushed Claire too far. He'd seen the spark of defiance in her eyes when he told her the business he needed to tend to wasn't suitable for a lady. She most likely suspected he was off enjoying himself with a mistress.

But what else could he do? Tell her the steward had been dishonest in how he handled the funds? Tell her the steward had made some gambling bets with Lord Hedwrett and couldn't pay everything back at once without arousing Nate's suspicions? Tell her that Lord Hedwrett refused to be paid back in installments?

He sighed. He should have taken the time to check the ledger after his brother died. But how could he have known the steward embezzled the funds? The steward had been a trusted servant. He'd handled the finances while both his father and brother lived. No one suspected any foul play. Had Lord Hedwrett not contacted him directly, he wouldn't have been the wiser. Well, he was wiser now, and now that he'd settled the debts the steward had made, he could wipe the slate clean and start over.

He glanced out his carriage window. It wasn't even dawn yet. The night was taking too long to pass. He shifted in the carriage seat. Maybe he should have stayed at another inn, but he was tired of traveling. Day after day, he ran from one place to another. All he wanted to do was go home to his comfortable bed and sleep for a year.

He groaned and peered up at the sky, trying to determine how early it was. Not even a hint of light was in the sky, which meant he had little else to do but think. Though he was exhausted, he couldn't sleep. He had drifted off to sleep as soon as he got in the carriage, but he had a dream that he and Claire had a son, and the son was asking her who he was and she told him he was his father. Then his son asked what a father was. At that point, Nate woke up and hadn't been able to get back to sleep since.

Claire wasn't with child, so there was no son to ask who he was. He fully intended to be in his children's lives. For sure, he had to teach his sons how to handle the affairs of the estate in case their stewards were dishonest with the finances.

He drummed his fingers on the seat and glanced out the window again. Still no light signaling that dawn would soon be coming. He shook his head and gritted his teeth.

Claire was mad at him. He knew it. She hadn't argued with him, but there was no denying that the last time he saw her, her furrowed eyebrows, thin lips, and piercing gaze were the mark of a lady who detested him. Even on their wedding day when she argued with him as soon as they reached the townhouse, she hadn't looked at him that way.

It wouldn't hurt to go home and talk to Claire, to make an effort to work out a compromise where they could both be happy, or at least content. He wasn't an unreasonable person, and she probably wasn't either, given the chance. He sighed and got as comfortable as he could in the seat. By the end of that hour, he was finally able to doze back off to sleep.

Chapter Fourteen

*A*fter breakfast the next morning, Claire scanned the hallway outside her bedchamber. Good. No one was in sight. She stepped out of the room and hurried to the corridor that would take her to the servants' staircase. Her heart was pounding so fast in her chest she thought it might burst. Thankfully, Mister Robinson had followed through on his word and left the clothes behind the stairs.

It took her longer to dress in stableboy clothes than she thought it would. The binding around her chest had to be secure, and without Marion's help, it proved to be a difficult task. But she managed through it, and one would be hard pressed to know she had breasts. Though Mister Robinson suggested she cut her hair, she couldn't bear the thought of doing so and settled for pinning it up and putting one of his hats over it. It wasn't perfect. She knew she looked like a youth instead of a gentleman due to her slight build and no facial hair, but it would be good enough. As long as she didn't let anyone see her up close, it could work.

She slipped out the back door and hurried to the stable, giving a quick scan of the area. Assured no one saw her, she pressed forward. By the time she made it to the stable, Mister Robinson waved for her to wait by the side of the building. She obeyed. As she waited, she caught sight of a carriage driving toward the house. She narrowed her eyes and tried to determine whose carriage it was. From a distance it was hard to tell. She wasn't told to expect anyone for a visit.

The carriage rounded a bend, giving her a clear view of it as it passed a row of trees. She gasped. It couldn't be! But it was. It was Roderick's carriage! She'd recognize the self-important 'R' on the crest on the carriage door anywhere. The carriage was still a ways off, but she didn't want him to see her, even if she was sure she passed off as a regular stableboy from this distance.

She faced away from the carriage and crept around the stable, trying to look as natural as possible so as not to arouse suspicion. Her heartbeat had gone from a trot to a hearty gallop. There was no way she could leave with Lord Roderick around. Maybe he forgot something and would be gone soon.

She lowered the hat over her eyes and bypassed another stableboy, grunting a greeting in the same manner he did. When she reached the stable door, she peered into it and saw Mister Robinson heading in her direction. Since the stable master's back was turned to her, she hurried into the stable and bolted for one of the empty stalls. My goodness but her heart was still beating furiously. This whole thing just might kill her unless she could get a grip on her nerves!

Mister Robinson hurried over to her. "What's wrong?"

Making sure the stable master wasn't looking in their direction, she whispered, "Lord Roderick's here!"

"Really?" He got ready to run to the door of the stable, but she grabbed his shirt and stopped him. "What is it?"

"I have to get back into the house without anyone seeing me."

"Why? Do you think he's going to look for you?"

"Yes. No. I don't know. Maybe." Who knew what her husband wanted to do?

"I should find out what's going on. At least we'll know what to do if I investigate."

Despite her apprehension, she nodded. It was probably her safest bet. As Mister Robinson left the stable, she glanced at the stable master who was talking to another stableboy. Neither one of them noticed her. She checked for another place she might hide, but she didn't see a suitable location. When one of them glanced her way, she ducked and prayed he hadn't seen her. Since no one called out to her, she figured she was safe in the empty stall, at least for the moment.

***

"Lord Roderick!"

Nate turned to his flustered butler who hurried out of the house. Curious, Nate turned from the carriage and straightened the collar of his tailcoat. "Is something wrong?"

"If I might have a word with you in private, my lord?"

Sensing the urgency in his butler's voice, Nate nodded and dismissed the coachman who hopped back on the carriage and drove it to a stable. "What is it?"

"I don't know how to tell you this, but it appears Lady Roderick has taken it upon herself to dress as a stableboy and go to the," he shrugged, "stable."

"Why would she do something so absurd?"

"I don't know. I saw her leaving the house from the servant quarters."

Goodness. Did being out here by herself without companionship make his wife go insane? Perhaps she'd done it out of desperation, maybe to see her family? If so, she was unbelievably naïve if she thought traveling alone as a stableboy would protect her from danger. He shook his head. His wife had a lot to learn about the more unpleasant aspects of the world, and quite frankly, he preferred it if she didn't have to learn them at all.

He followed the butler's gaze to the stable. With a long sigh, he debated the best course of action before he spoke. "In light of Lady Roderick's good name, I think it's best if no one discusses what's happened."

"Of course, my lord."

"Thank you. I'll make sure you and the others are compensated for your kindness when it comes time to pay your salary."

"Thank you, my lord."

The matter settled, Nate headed straight for the stable, his gaze going to Mister Robinson as he jogged his way. He frowned. What could Mister Robinson be up to? By the smirk on the youth's arrogant face, Nate surmised that whatever mischief the ward was up to, it couldn't be to his advantage. Pressing forward, he didn't bother to slow down when Mister Robinson intercepted him.

"Lord Roderick," the youth began, sounding far more jovial than he had a right to be.

"I don't have time for idle chatter, Mister Robinson. I have an important matter to tend to. If you're bored, I suggest you muck out a stall."

Though Mister Robinson gave a slight grimace, his tone remained cheerful. "Oh, I'll clean the stalls. I've been doing it ever since I got here."

"All right."

"I wanted your opinion, my lord."

"On what?" Nate tried to hide the irritation in his voice.

"On…on…" He glanced around the area and pointed to a group of shrubs. "Those, my lord. Since I've been diligently shoveling horse manure, can I trim those?"

Diligently shoveling horse manure? To hear the stable master speak, Mister Robinson had to be constantly reminded to tend to his task since he'd often been caught staring off into space, daydreaming about his illicit activities no doubt. With a shake of his head, Nate gave a firm, "No."

Mister Robinson grunted and then stepped in front of him.

Startled, Nate stopped in his tracks and stared at the insolent youth. "Mister Robinson, I suggest you get out of my way. I am heading to the stable."

"Yes, I know, but I think I can do a better job of trimming those shrubs than the gardener."

"You're here to tend to the stable, not the shrubs." Nate took a step to the side, and Mister Robinson followed suit. Irritated, he said, "I demand you stop this nonsense at once."

"But why? You haven't given me a good reason. I insist you tell me why I can't trim the shrubs."

"Because I'm the owner of this estate. You don't need a better reason than that."

Mister Robinson opened his mouth and then shut it.

Good. That shut him up. Glaring at him, he stepped around him and strode toward the stables.

"Oh!" Mister Robinson exclaimed. "I think something important came for you today. Earlier today. Before you arrived."

Surprised at what he knew to be an outright lie—and a bad one at that, Nate paused and faced him. "Something important?"

"Yes, my lord. It was a large trunk."

"That's odd. Why didn't my butler inform me of this when I was talking to him?"

"I'm sure he meant to, but he most have forgotten about it."

"Then it can't be that important, can it?"

Mister Robinson glanced at the stable and let out a nervous laugh. "Of course, it can be important. You should see what's in it."

"I don't have time for this."

"But it's important!"

Nate narrowed his eyes at him. Just what was the youth up to? He seemed surprisingly adamant that Nate not go to the stable. Nate glanced at the stable his wife was in—dressed up as a stableboy—and then back at Perry's mischievous ward. "I'll see it in due time." He resumed his walk to the stable, this time at a hurried pace.

As he suspected, the youth began to stammer something about forgetting to blow out the candles in his room, and if Nate was right, Mister Robinson claimed to have lit a hundred of them. But he hardly heard the other items the youth was rambling on about. Anything Perry's ward was saying was nonsense. And perhaps that nonsense was supposed to be a distraction. A distraction from what? He couldn't have had a hand in Claire dressing up in boy's clothes so she could run off to London, could he?

The closer to the stable Nate got, the angrier he became. Just what business did Mister Robinson have in talking Claire into this scheme? Didn't he realize the potential danger he was putting her into? Or was he being as careless as he had the night he almost challenged the Duke of Watkins to a duel and almost lost his head? The youth had no sense of responsibility.

By the time they reached the stable, Mister Robinson looked like he was ready to panic, and that only served to increase Nate's suspicions. Ignoring the youth who made an attempt to block his entrance, he entered the stable and scanned the area for a very feminine looking stableboy. But the only people he saw were his coachman and the stable master.

They turned to him, and the stable master approached him. "My lord, may I help you?"

He scanned the length of the stable, not bothering to pay an anxious Mister Robinson any mind. His wife had to be in here somewhere...unless she managed to slip out of the stable while he was walking here. But there was nowhere she could hide on her way back to the house. All that spanned between here and the house was grass. She had to be in here. He peered around Mister Robinson who made it a point to shuffle back and forth.

That was it! Nate had all he could take of Perry's ward. There was no doubt about it. The youth had a part in his wife dressing up as a stableboy. He turned to the coachman. "Please escort Mister Robinson back into the house and acquaint him with his new duty of cleaning the chamber pots."

Mister Robinson's jaw dropped. "Cleaning chamber pots? You can't mean to give me that job!"

Pulling himself to his full height, he lowered his gaze to a scared ward. "The chambermaid is relieved of her duties until you can figure out what responsibility means."

Before the youth could protest, the coachman hurried to lead him out of the stable. Glad to be done with that nuisance, he turned in the stable master's direction when he caught sight of a horse that snorted and moved away from the stall next to it. His eyes narrowed as he tried to get a good view of the empty stall next to the horse. Though he couldn't be sure, he suspected Claire was hiding there.

Turning to the stable master, he whispered, "Play along."

Though the stable master looked confused, he nodded.

Nate headed for the empty stall. When he reached it, he opened the door and saw a person hunched in the corner. "Pardon me?"

The person stiffened but didn't look up.

"My name is Lord Roderick, and I happen to own this stable. Who are you?"

When the person looked up at him, he didn't know whether to laugh or roll his eyes in exasperation that Claire actually believed she passed for a stableboy. Anyone could tell she was a lady! He waited for her to speak, but she seemed unable to. In fact, it seemed all she could do was look at him with wide eyes, knowing full well she'd been caught but not being able to do anything about it. He cleared his throat and motioned for her to leave the stall. She hesitated, her gaze going from him to the spot next to him and back to him.

"I see no reason for you to hide in a stall on your first day of employment," he finally said, giving the stable master an expectant glance.

Quick to oblige, the stable master stepped forward and nodded. "The new stableboy arrived today, my lord. I believe his name is…Mister Henry."

"Is that your name, lad?" Nate asked, noting Claire's wide eyes.

"Uh…" Claire glanced from one to the other.

"I'm afraid he's a bit on the shy side," the stable master replied.

"Apparently." Nate clapped his hands together, intentionally startling her, and motioned to one of the horses. "Your first task is to get my horse ready. I'll return to the house and change into proper attire. When I get back, I expect my horse to be ready to go for a ride." He made a turn, as if to leave, but snapped his fingers and turned back to her, stepping close enough so she had to back up.

She backed up into the stall and nearly tripped.

He caught her by the arm before she fell and chuckled. "My goodness, lad, but you spook easily." He let go of her arm when she was steady on her feet. "I only meant to tell you to get another horse ready."

"A-an-another horse?" she squeaked.

"Yes. I intend to show you around. Being new here, you need to get acquainted with the place."

Before she could respond, he hurried out of the stable, careful not to break out into a full laugh until he was out of her hearing distance.

Chapter Fifteen

Claire fumbled through the process of getting the horses ready. Fortunately, the stable master helped her.

"I wish I would have known you were due to arrive today," he said as he showed her how to strap the saddle in place. "I knew we were due for a new stableboy but expected him next week."

"I...I thought it was today," she mumbled, looking away from him in case he figured out she wasn't this new stableboy who was due to work here. She didn't even know one was expected here, but it wasn't like she kept track of such things so who was she to question it?

"You have nothing to worry about. Lord Roderick is as good as they come. This is a good place to work."

"Yes, I heard," she muttered. Who hadn't sung her husband's praises as if he were some kind of saint? Truly, her husband couldn't be more annoying. He was pleasant to everyone but her—and Mister Robinson.

"All right then." He finished the task and patted the horse's neck. "He's a beauty, isn't he?"

She shrugged. A horse was a horse. There seemed to be little difference between one or the other, except maybe for their color.

"This one over here will be yours for today," he called out as he headed for a stall to her right.

Curious to see which horse she'd be riding, she followed him and saw the light brown mare.

He led the mare out of the stall and gestured to the other saddle. "Go ahead and put it on, just like I showed you over there."

She glanced at Roderick's horse and then back at her own. Despite her apprehension, she went over to the saddle which had been placed on the bench. She picked it up and nearly fell back. Good gracious, this thing was heavier than it looked!

"Buck up there, lad. You can do it," he encouraged. "It'll do you some good to put some muscle on those bones."

She winced as she steadied herself. Putting some muscles on her bones wasn't something she particularly wanted to do. But she was trapped and had to follow through with this stupid idea. Who was to know such a clever plan could backfire on her like this? She actually succeeded in passing off as a stableboy, but she was no closer to getting to London than she had been the day she got here. Curse her husband for his uncanny timing. Only he would show up as she was about to finally make her escape.

She reached her horse and managed to throw the saddle over it. Unfortunately, it slipped right off the mare's back and onto the ground.

The stable master chuckled. "Yes, you definitely need to build some strength in those arms." He picked the saddle up and, without any effort she could see, got the saddle in place on the animal. "Go on and secure it."

She took a deep breath and did the best she could, hoping she recalled his instructions right so she wouldn't further embarrass herself. She managed through the process with less finesse than she cared to admit, and he had to help a couple of times before everything was done. After that, he showed her how to put the bridles on the horses.

Just as they were fitting the reins, Roderick entered the stable. Her stomach twisted up into knots. It was bad enough being around him when she was dressed up as herself, but as a stableboy, it somehow seemed worse.

"Are we ready?" Roderick asked, stopping right in front of her with what seemed to be an amused grin on his face.

Unsure of what to make by his expression, she shrugged and mumbled, "Yes, Lord Roderick." She nearly gagged on saying his name that way, but it was how a stableboy would refer to him, so what choice did she have? She reached the side of her horse and put her foot in the stirrup.

He stood by his horse and cleared his throat.

With a start, she turned her head in his direction.

"I require your assistance, Mister Henry," Roderick said.

She scanned him up and down. "With what?"

The stable master grinned, but Roderick spoke up, pulling her attention back to him. "I need help getting on the horse."

She frowned. "Haven't you ridden a horse before?"

"Of course, I have, but nonetheless, I need your help," he insisted, motioning to the stirrup.

Resisting the urge to sigh, she went over to him and inspected the stirrup. What could possibly be wrong with it? "It looks fine, my lord, unless you mean for me to wipe it clean for you?" Perhaps he needed everything to be perfectly clean before he went riding.

"Not that. I need you to help me up."

"What?"

The stable master cleared his throat and headed off to who-knew-where. Was he laughing because she was inept at this job?

"Well?"

She turned her attention back to Roderick. "You're an adult. Can't you get yourself on the horse?"

"Are you or are you not acquainted with your duties?" Roderick asked.

It was on the tip of her tongue to argue that it was ridiculous someone of her smaller stature should help him onto a horse, but she was playing a part. "Very well. What do you want me to do?"

"Put my foot in the stirrup."

She stopped herself from rolling her eyes and leaned forward so she could grab his foot. After she slipped it into the stirrup, she started walking to her horse when he cleared his throat again. Spinning around, she asked, "What now?"

"I require further assistance."

Her jaw dropped. He couldn't be serious! What would he want next? For her to carry him into the house?

"Mister Henry, I'd like to show you the property before dinner."

Grumbling under her breath, she went back to him.

"Good. Give me the reins."

She did as instructed and waited to see what else he might demand.

"Place my hands on the saddle," he said.

"You can't put your hands up there yourself?" she asked in disbelief.

"Sure, I can, but I'm an earl so I have no need to do this myself."

She stared at him for a long moment, wondering if he was teasing or being serious. She thought she saw his lips curl up for a moment on his otherwise stoic face, but she couldn't be sure.

"Mister Henry?" he pressed.

"All right, all right." She took his hands and plopped them on the saddle. "There. Are we done yet?"

"No. Now you need to boost me."

"Boost you?"

"Yes. Push me up by my rear end."

"Your what?"

He turned away from her and jutted his rear end out. "Place your hands on my behind and push me up."

She stood still, not able to move. She couldn't imagine touching him—or anyone—in such a private area. Was this really something stableboys did for their employers?

"This position is rather awkward," Roderick said. "Please hurry up."

Face flushed, she stepped away from him and shook her head. "I cannot."

"Why not? It is your job."

"But...but..." She shook her head and hurried back to her horse. "I'm sorry, my lord, but I can't do anything that makes me uncomfortable."

He let out a disappointed sigh. "I'll let this instance pass, but I suggest you get used to doing your job, regardless of the details involved in it."

She watched as he got into the saddle with surprising ease. Why would he want help into the saddle when it was obvious he could do it himself? Were earls really that lazy?

"Can you get on the horse?" Roderick called out.

"Sure, I can. I'm a stableboy," she replied, hoping she sounded appropriately offended that he'd even have to ask.

"Or so you would make it seem."

She eyed him suspiciously. Did he suspect the truth?

"Come on, lad. Get on your horse."

In the past, she'd always had help on a horse, and she'd always had a sidesaddle. She didn't think it possible, but this was going to be far more awkward than almost having to touch Roderick's read end. She grabbed the saddle, put a foot in the stirrup, and made an attempt to get in the saddle. Unfortunately, she failed and stumbled to find the ground with her free foot.

Ignoring Roderick as he laughed, she tried again. This time she made it on the saddle, though she had to wiggle her way into a good position. The horse snorted, as if mocking her efforts. She sighed. Granted, she looked ridiculous. She sure felt ridiculous! But she didn't exactly appreciate the reminder.

"Good," Roderick said, looking pleased. "Now we can be on our way."

He nudged the horse in the sides with his feet and the animal headed out of the stable. She imitated his actions and was rewarded as her mare lurched after Roderick. She gripped the reins in her hands. Goodness but riding a horse with her legs indecently spread apart was proving to be a challenge! She adjusted her hips to balance her swaying body the best she could. Up ahead, Roderick stopped and waited for her. It took her longer to catch up to him than she preferred, but she didn't dare go faster in case she slipped off the saddle.

"Good heavens, lad," Roderick called out. "You're in no hurry to do anything, are you?"

"I'm going as fast as I can," she replied through gritted teeth.

"Mind your disposition."

"I'm trying to keep my balance on this thing. I'm not snapping at you."

"You're trying to keep your balance? Aren't you proficient on a horse?"

"I haven't ridden one in a while."

And that wasn't too far from the truth. She hadn't ridden one in a year, and even then she'd been sitting side saddle and going at a leisurely pace. Roderick, it seemed, wanted to go into a full trot. When she caught up to him, she fully expected him to speed up, but to her surprise, he slowed his pace so he could stay beside her. They rode for a good ten minutes up a slight incline before he spoke to her.

"So," Roderick began with a glance in her direction, "what brings you to Weston?"

"Employment." Why else would a stableboy be in a stable?

"But why Weston? Why not Camden or Valentine?"

She shrugged. "I don't know. It just seemed like the right place to be."

"So you picked this place at random? On a whim?"

"Yes. It seemed like a good idea," she ventured, hoping he'd let the matter drop.

He pulled the reins on the horse to a stop, and she followed suit. "This is the best view of Weston you'll find from anywhere on this property."

Up to now, she hadn't been paying attention to her surroundings. She'd been focused on keeping her balance on the horse. Now, however, she took the time to look around her and noted the lush green landscape dotted with trees. A pond was to her right and the manor was to her left, and there were flowers spread throughout the area. Her eyes went to the gazebo and path she walked almost every day. It was the one place where she felt at peace. From a distance, it was a lovely view.

"What do you think?" he asked.

"It's beautiful," she admitted.

"Unfortunately, my wife doesn't like it."

Her eyes wide, she looked at him, wondering why he'd be telling a stableboy something so personal. "My lord, I don't think it's my place to know what Lady Roderick thinks."

He shrugged. "If I can't tell you, then who can I tell?"

"Do you make it a point to tell all of the servants about your wife?"

"No. Just you."

"Why?"

"Why not?"

She inwardly groaned. It was irritating that he answered her question with another question.

"My wife wishes to return to London," Roderick continued. "Up to this point, I've been telling her no, but I'm wondering if I should agree. I'm starting to think I've been too quick to judge her. I've ignored her ever since we got married.

Well, there were a couple of times when we talked, but we spent that time arguing. It's not the best way to start a marriage."

Her cheeks grew warm. Why was he telling a stableboy all of this? "My lord, I must insist that you refrain from telling me anything else. What happens between you and your wife is none of my concern."

"I think it concerns you very much."

"No, it doesn't. I'm just a stableboy."

He shot her a pointed look. "You detest me so much that you'll disguise yourself as a stableboy and risk endangering your life to travel to London alone?"

Her shoulders dropped. He knew. "I didn't see any other way to go to London. I'm tired of being here all by myself without anyone to keep me company, and before you say it, though I love Marion dearly, it's not the same thing as having my family around. Despite what you think, I'm not a cold-hearted lady whose sole pleasure in life is money. I want companionship. Companionship from someone who is my equal."

His expression softening, he said, "I'm sorry, Claire. I should've been more attentive to you. I should have brought you out here sooner and showed you the estate and helped you adjust to being its mistress. I was just…"

She studied his expression and knew he was struggling to find the right words. Deciding to say it for him, she spoke up in a soft voice, "You assumed something about me that wasn't true."

He sighed, seeming to want to believe her but afraid to. "For the past couple of weeks, my attention was required elsewhere. You inquired about the urgent business I needed to tend to, but I wouldn't disclose it. Well, I'll do so now. It turns out the steward was embezzling funds. He didn't do it while my father lived but for reasons he won't disclose, he decided to start three years ago when my brother became the earl. I didn't find out until I received a letter from Lord Hedwrett demanding the money owed him. I did some investigating and realized what was going on. It turned out the steward dug a substantial hole for me. I've been running all over the place to make sure people are happy and the finances are balanced."

"I'm sorry," she whispered.

"It's not what you thought you'd get yourself into when you married me. The problem is that even though a gentleman might have a title, it doesn't mean he can spend money all the time. That's certainly true for me now."

He sighed and rubbed his eyes, and for the first time since they married, her heart went out to him. He hadn't slept well, that much was evident by the bags under his eyes and his drooping shoulders. It must have been humbling to have to admit he didn't have the funds she'd assumed he did.

"I have everything I need," she softly told him. "You don't have to worry I'll spend anything."

"I didn't realize at the time we married what was going on, but if I had and told you, would you have married me?"

"I didn't want to marry you regardless, so no, I wouldn't have chosen to marry you. Even if your steward hadn't left you with debts, I wouldn't have chosen you. My father saw fit to make sure I had to marry you, so here we are." She shrugged. "However, you don't need to worry. Now that I know the situation, I'll act accordingly."

"Thank you."

Unsure of what else to say, she nodded.

"I haven't had a thing to eat since yesterday evening," he finally said after a long silence passed between them. "Mind if we continue this discussion in the house?"

"No, I don't mind."

They headed back for the stable, and this time the silence that descended between them didn't seem so awkward.

Chapter Sixteen

Claire brushed her hair after she put on a purple dress, her anxious strokes revealing her apprehension. It wasn't that Roderick had been mean to her just now, but since she hadn't talked to him—*really* talked to him, she couldn't fight back the butterflies fluttering wildly in her stomach.

Marion hurried into the room. "My lady, let me do that."

She didn't realize her hands were trembling until she handed Marion the brush. She sat in front of the mirror and tried to relax, but her nervousness prevented her from doing so. She had a good chance to finally get through to Roderick, and as long as she was careful, she wouldn't ruin it.

Glancing at her reflection in the mirror, she watched as Marion's skilled fingers pinned her hair up in an attractive style. If she wasn't so nervous, she'd engage in a conversation with the older lady. But she couldn't focus on anything except what she was going to tell Roderick.

"All done," Marion said as she took out Claire's favorite necklace. "Would you like to wear this today?"

Claire figured she might as well so she nodded and waited for her to clasp the sapphire necklace around her neck.

"Everything will be fine, my lady," Marion whispered and patted her shoulder in a reassuring manner. "Sometimes a kind word can work wonders."

Claire watched as she left the room. She wondered how much Marion knew about what was going on. It wasn't Marion's way to pry, but she did observe things from a distance. No doubt she had to suspect Claire did something to mess up her hair after she'd pinned it up that morning before breakfast. But to her credit, she kept quiet and wasn't the type to gossip, something Claire was grateful for, especially today.

Now, however, it wasn't time to think of what Marion might or might not know about her dressing up as a stableboy. She needed to talk to Roderick. Taking a deep breath, she stood up and lumbered out of the room and down the steps. She wasn't sure what to expect from talking to him, but as long as she could see her family, then that's what mattered. When she reached the drawing room, she saw that he was at her desk, studying the papers she'd been drawing on. She rushed over to stop him, but he was too quick for her.

"What are these?" he asked with an amused smile.

She couldn't tell if he was amused that she was trying to get the papers back or if he was amused at her drawings. Since she couldn't reach high enough to get the papers from him, she forced her hands at her sides and groaned. "They're to pass the time."

"Time?" He sorted through the papers. "These don't look like clocks to me."

"I said they're to 'pass the time', not pictures of 'time'. They aren't clocks. They're flowers."

His eyebrows furrowed and he studied them. "Flowers?"

"Yes. These are the petals, these are the stems, and these are the leaves." She pointed to the items as she listed them off and noticed the way he squinted, as if he was having trouble picking them out. With a sigh, she added, "I didn't say they were well-drawn flowers. They're just the flowers I saw while walking to the gazebo."

"Is that why you spent so much time studying them?"

"You've seen me on my walks?" she asked, surprised.

He shrugged. "I happened to notice you while riding my horse."

Unexpectedly pleased he had, indeed, noticed her, she cleared her throat. "I happen to enjoy drawing, even if I'm no good at it."

He handed the papers back to her. "I'm sure you can draw other things well."

"No, I can't. My best work involves flowers."

She noted the slight curl at the corner of his lips and knew he was struggling to hold in his laughter for her sake. "I know I'm not good at drawing."

"I didn't say you weren't good at it."

"There's no need to lie to me. I can handle the truth."

The butler came in and set the tray on the table by the settee and chairs. Glad for the reprieve from discussing her artistic ability, or rather a lack thereof, she motioned to the settee. After he left her desk, she put the papers in the drawer, retrieved her sister's letter, and followed him, not surprised he chose to stand by the chair instead of standing next to the settee.

"You wish to discuss that letter?" Roderick asked her.

Forcing her mind back to him, she handed the letter to him and sat down. He eased into the chair and opened it.

"Yes. It's from my sister," she began as she poured tea into their cups. "We've been invited to London."

He read through the letter and grimaced. "Tell me she doesn't really want to marry Lord Hedwrett."

"Why? What else is there to know besides the fact that your steward owes him money?"

He sighed and handed it back to her. "You don't want to know. Such things aren't suitable for a lady's ears."

She glanced at the paper in her hands and wondered what Lord Hedwrett could possibly be like. From the grim tone in

Roderick's voice, she wondered how worried she should be about her sister.

Roderick picked up his cup and sipped it. "I don't feel comfortable discussing certain things about Hedwrett, but suffice it to say your sister shouldn't marry him. Try to talk her out of it if you can, but if she does marry him, I can't let you visit her without me. There's no telling what he'd do."

She swallowed the sweet tea and nodded. "You've told me enough to know he's not the best gentleman for her. Mister Morris asked her to marry him, but," she shrugged, "to be honest, she didn't want him because he didn't have a title or enough money. So yes, she values such things more than I do, but that doesn't mean I don't love her. I'd like to see her again."

He finished drinking his tea and held onto the cup while studying her. "You will. I promise."

She took another sip of her tea. As long as he was willing to work with her, she figured she might as well ask other things that were troubling her. "When will I get to see you for more than minutes at a time?"

"I'm surprised you want to see me at all."

"Even if our marriage isn't ideal, it'd be nice if I knew my own husband."

"I'm sorry I've been neglecting you. We'll set out for London tomorrow so you can see your family. While we're there, we can also spend some time together. In fact, we should start spending time together today. Then we can get to know each other. What do you think?"

"I'd like that," she admitted. "And I won't go shopping with my sister."

He gave a nod to indicate he understood before he drank more of his tea.

A long moment passed as she debated to ask the thing that was nagging at her the most, but she had to know. Even if it was something she didn't want to hear, she needed to know. "Are you seeing a mistress?"

"Pardon me?"

"I know it's common for gentlemen in your position to do such things, and I wanted to know if you do as well." Not that she wanted him to, but what could she do to stop him? She figured she was better off knowing if he did. That way she could keep enough distance from him so he didn't end up hurting her.

"No, I don't have a mistress. I never have and I never will."

She breathed a sigh of relief.

"I assure you my time away from home was spent on making sure my steward's debtors were adequately paid. I can't say I enjoyed meeting them, but it was a necessary evil."

She nodded and drank the tea, enjoying its warmth.

"While we're in London, we can go to Hyde Park for a horse ride or a walk. Or if you'd prefer, we can visit a museum, see a balloon launch, or go to the theatre."

"You'll do these things with me?" she asked.

"Of course." He sighed and touched her knee, surprising her. "I haven't been fair to you. I need to take time to know you."

She smiled. "I'd like that."

He checked his pocket watch and stood up, holding his hand out to her. "I'm afraid I haven't eaten yet. Would you keep me company while I do so, Lady Roderick?"

Shocked that he referred to her as *Lady Roderick*, she stared at him, unable to determine what to say.

"Is that a no?"

Forcing aside her surprise, she put her cup on the tray and stood up. "No. Yes. I mean, yes. I'll be happy to keep you company during the meal."

He smiled and extended his arm to her.

Still surprised, but pleased, by his change of heart, she accepted his arm and went to the dining room with him.

***

Nate glanced up from his baked eggs. Across from him, Claire ate some fruit. Both of them had changed after coming into the house, and he was relieved to see her wearing a dress again. Though he was tired from his lack of sleep the night before, he was also happy. Today seemed to be the turning point for him and his wife. He felt much better now that he'd taken the time to talk to her. Really talk to her. And though he'd never admit it, he should have taken Perry's advice sooner.

Clearing his throat, he said, "Would you like to take a walk after we eat?"

"Yes. It'll be nice to have some company for a change."

"If you want to take some paper along, you can draw the things you see during the walk."

She took a sip of her tea and offered a slight smile. "I could do that, but then you couldn't guess what the drawings are supposed to be."

Surprised she had a sense of humor, he grinned. "I bet I could. There's a gazebo where we can sit. Let's go there, and when you draw something, I'll guess what it is."

"That doesn't sound very interesting."

"Then how would you make it interesting?"

She shrugged. "I don't know."

He ate his last portion of eggs and swallowed the rest of his tea before he wiped his mouth with a cloth napkin and straightened his back. "I have an idea. If I'm correct about what you draw, you have to do whatever I want, and if I'm wrong, I have to do anything you want."

"I could lie. I could say I didn't draw whatever you guess."

"When I made the suggestion, I assumed you'd act honorably, but if you prefer mischief, then I suggest you write down what you draw before I guess. That way I can be sure you aren't trying to get me to do your bidding."

She bit her lower lip. "What kind of things would we have to do for each other?"

Amused at her worried tone, he said, "Nothing embarrassing. Perhaps you could have me draw something. Then you can see how badly I can draw."

"You tried your hand at art?"

"Not necessarily art, but I've scribbled on occasion when I was bored."

"Scribbled?"

He shrugged. "I didn't try to draw anything in particular."

"Oh."

He studied her as she finished the strawberries on the plate. "You're disappointed?"

She wiped her mouth with the napkin and set it on the table. "No. All right, a little. I thought Lord Clement was exaggerating when he said you were serious all the time."

"He told you I'm serious?"

"All the time," she emphasized.

Though her tone was grim, he detected a twinkle in her eye. Intrigued, he motioned to the footman that they were done with breakfast. "I suppose we'll see how accurate he is when we take that walk. Bring your drawing pad."

Once she collected her drawing pad and graphite pencil, they went outside. As they started down the path that would take them to the south side of the manor, he breathed in the fresh air, noting it was an ideal day for a walk. The sun was out, the clouds white and fluffy, and the air cool enough to enjoy the day.

He caught sight of a rabbit hopping along the grounds and turned to his wife. "What about him?"

She stopped walking. "Who?"

"That rabbit. Have you ever tried to draw animals?"

A slight grimace crossed her face. "Yes. Not successfully. I told you flowers are my best work."

"I remember you saying that, but truly, how bad can you be?" Considering how bad she was at drawing flowers, he didn't think she could do much worse.

"You don't want to know," she mumbled and continued her walk.

Following her until he caught up to her, he said, "You can't know what I want or don't want to know. Maybe I really want to see you draw a rabbit."

"You'll laugh at it."

He chuckled. "Why don't you draw one when we get to the gazebo, and I'll see if I can guess that's what it is?"

"But you already know what it is because you're asking me to draw it."

"I didn't say to make it your first drawing. Just draw it at some point. If you are as bad as you say, then I won't be able to pick out which one it is." She seemed to be considering it, so he added, "I'll try to draw one, too."

Her eyebrows rose. "You will?"

"Yes, and I promise to do my best. I won't be scribbling."

"All right."

They reached the flowers, and when she came to a stop, she bent to study them. Perhaps he should have suggested that she kneel instead since she was showing him, and anyone else who happened to be in the area, a nice view of her backside. He quickly looked around to make sure no one was in sight, and since no one was, he decided to keep quiet. She was his wife, after all, and there was no harm in him enjoying this view of her. It wasn't like he hadn't already seen her naked.

His mind unwittingly went to their wedding night when she'd taken off her clothes in front of him. With all the running around he'd done to get the estate back in good standing, he hadn't thought much of that night, but now that he was spending time with her, he could think about it. And really, it wasn't as if thinking about it was painful. No, in fact it was very pleasant. His lips curled up into a smile. He might do well to think of it often.

"What's your favorite color?"

It took him a moment to realize she was asking him a question. Forcing his eyes off of her bottom, he made eye contact with her. "Pardon?"

"What's your favorite color?"

"Oh, let's see." At the moment, it was purple because that was the color of her dress, and the dress brought out her curves in a way that delighted him. But he couldn't tell her that. Clearing his throat, he said, "Black."

She straightened up, a process that disappointed him since it meant he no longer had a good view of her backside. "Black?"

"Sure. It's a color."

"But none of these flowers are black."

"Did you mean what my favorite color for a flower is?"

She nodded.

And that right there showed just how little he was paying attention to what she'd been saying. Though embarrassed to be caught not listening to her, he shrugged. "I suppose red is doable for a flower, but to be honest, thinking of flowers isn't something gentlemen do."

"I suppose not. Flowers are something ladies enjoy."

"Right." However, since she was interested in them, he should probably take some interest in them as well. "Which color do you like best?"

"I can't decide between purple or yellow."

"Purple."

"Purple?"

Glancing at her dress, he nodded. "Purple."

She smiled and shrugged. "All right. Purple it is." She picked a purple wildflower.

"Are you going to draw that?"

"No. You are when you can't guess what I draw."

"So sure of yourself, are you?" he asked, finding the challenge more delightful than he supposed it should be. This challenge, after all, had nothing to do with politics or the war, and it didn't have a chessboard involved. But he caught a playfully competitive edge to her disposition and found it pleased him, so he was more than happy to go along with whatever she had planned.

She shrugged in a coy way that excited him and said, "You couldn't tell I had drawn flowers, so yes, I am sure of myself."

Further intrigued, he countered, "Perhaps I really knew you'd drawn flowers but wanted to amuse you."

"No, that wasn't the case."

"But how can you be sure?"

"Because I saw the look on your face when you saw those pictures. I'd never seen a gentleman who struggled more to control the urge to laugh. It was actually kind of you to regard my feelings the way you did."

It was funny she should term it that way. He hadn't thought of it as being anything chivalrous, but he rather fancied the way she termed it. In a way, it made him feel like a hero.

"Are you ready to go to the gazebo?" she asked.

Sensing she looked forward to his ability to guess what she drew, he nodded, and they strolled to the white structure surrounded by bushes and trees. He couldn't recall a time he'd ever been here, and it impressed him it was well maintained.

"This is a beautiful place," she commented and stood still for a moment.

He stopped beside her so she could study it. She seemed to study almost everything she came across that she admired, but he supposed that was something ladies did. Spending time looking at flowers and gazebos wasn't really that much of a waste, especially when he was seeing a side of his wife he enjoyed. It reminded him of that brief moment on their wedding night when she'd confided her fears to him. It was nice to know she could be that way when she wasn't drunk.

Once she headed toward the gazebo, he joined her. He went up the steps behind her and sat next to her, something that seemed to startle her since she gave a slight jerk.

Chuckling, he teased, "You have no need to worry. I won't watch as you draw. I'll play this game honorably."

"No, it's not that. It's..."

"It's what?"

She hesitated, a worried frown on her lips. Finally, she shook her head. "Nothing. Shall we get started?"

He thought to press her, to find out what had disturbed her, but he figured she was entitled to keep her thoughts to herself and settled for nodding his agreement. She turned her attention to the drawing pad, the purple wildflower still in her hand. He wondered why she held onto it like she did. She couldn't mean to draw it. That would be too obvious.

With a shrug, he decided it was one of the quirky things ladies did and scanned their surroundings. He didn't note anything of particular interest. A few birds, the breeze wafting through the tree branches, and the way the cloud caused a shadow to fall across a section of the lawn. Nothing exciting, but he noted how peaceful everything was. With the activity in London, it was easy to forget life could slow down. And even more surprising was the fact that he didn't mind it.

Beside him, Claire finished her drawing and held it up to him. "What do you think this is?"

He bit his tongue so he wouldn't say the first thing that came to mind because it couldn't be right and he knew her delicate sensibilities would not permit her to draw such a thing. He blinked several times, willing the image of an erection between a pair of breasts from his mind. It wasn't that. There was no way it was that. And this only proved that accepting a book from

159

Lord Edon gave a gentleman mental images that would alarm a virginal wife.

He scanned the grounds again, trying to find something—anything—that might resemble what he'd seen. All he needed was to find two round objects and a pole. Surely, that couldn't be too hard. And yet, as he frantically tried to find anything similar to it, his luck failed him.

Resigned, he lied and said, "It looks like two balls and a stick." At that, he inwardly cringed. Likening a gentleman's erection to a stick, indeed. Clearing his throat, he added, "I mean a branch. One that's thick and long. Maybe even a tree. Yes, a big tree that dwarfs the bushes surrounding it." Yes, that sounded much better.

To his surprise, she let out a disappointed sigh. "How did you know?"

"I'm right?"

"Yes. I was drawing that tree over there, except I wouldn't say the tree dwarfs the bushes. The bushes are a good height."

"I'm sure they seem that way from your vantage point, but that tree is very big."

"There are other trees on the property that are bigger."

He gasped. "I should think not!"

"All right. I'll let you believe what you will."

He was ready to argue with her but reminded himself that she had no idea what he'd really seen in her drawing.

"What do you want me to do?" she asked.

"Do?"

"You guessed right about what I was drawing, so I have to do something you want."

Oh right. The interesting part of this morning's venture, though he had to admit taking time to enjoy the grounds and talking to her were turning out to be far more entertaining than he imagined they'd be. He thought for a moment on what he'd like her to do and then recalled how lovely she'd looked without her hair pinned up. "I'd like you to take those pins out of your hair."

She furrowed her eyebrows. "That's an odd request."

"Is it?"

"I don't see why you'd want such a thing."

"And what would you rather have me ask you to do?"

After a long moment, she shrugged and placed the pad on the bench. "You win."

Laughing as she started pulling the pins out, he asked, "I win?"

"Yes. I don't know what else you could have me do."

She was wrong about that. He could ask her to do plenty, but since they were in a public area where anyone could see them, he didn't dare.

She took out a few pins and held them to him. "Will you hold them for me? I don't want any to fall to the ground. They were a gift from my sister, and I'd hate to lose them."

"Yes." As she put them in his hand and picked out more from her hair, he studied the beaded pins which twinkled in the sunlight. "You miss your sister, don't you?"

"Terribly."

"Do you find any joy in being here?" he whispered, afraid of her answer but needing to know.

"I enjoy being here with you today," she softly admitted and then handed him the rest of the pins. "It was hard to be alone. I don't like being around a lot of people, but I like spending the day with someone whose company I enjoy."

"Isn't that true for everyone?"

"No, not my sister. She loves being surrounded by people."

"But she also likes being around you, I'm sure."

"She does, but when she is with me, she wants to go where's there's a lot of activity. She has a hard time sitting still unless she's watching a play. Something like what we're doing today would bore her. She'd say there's nothing to see out here."

Up until today, he would have agreed with her sister.

"Another reason why I don't like crowded areas is that I have a tendency to get faint. The ball was very uncomfortable for me. That's why I went out on the veranda. I was lightheaded and felt as if the walls were closing in on me."

"Really?"

She nodded. "I would have gotten my mother, but she was clear across the room, and I knew I'd faint if I didn't get outside soon."

"Oh." So that's why she'd been holding the column. She was supporting herself, and that meant she hadn't been out there in hopes of getting a titled gentleman to notice her. "I'm sorry I assumed the worst that night."

She smiled at him then, and for the life of him, he couldn't remember where they were. The rest of the world faded away, and all he could think of was how beautiful she looked. He reached out and touched her hair, noting its silky texture. Though her cheeks grew pink, she didn't look away from him as he ran his fingers through her hair in an attempt to comb it out so her waves framed her face.

"You're beautiful," he murmured, grateful it hadn't worked out with the Duke of Rumsey's daughter after all. Lady Catherine might have been pleasant enough, but he doubted he would have enjoyed being with her the same way he was enjoying his time with his wife. "I was wrong about you," he added, finally making eye contact with her. "You aren't the person I thought you were. I'm sorry I gave you so much grief when we first married."

Her smile widened, and in that instant, he knew everything was going to be good for them. She wouldn't hold a grudge. She was offering a chance to start over, and he appreciated that. He cupped the side of her face in his hand and leaned forward so he could kiss her. Her lips were as soft and warm as he remembered, but this kiss was much better than the one they'd shared on their wedding night. This time she wasn't drunk. She knew what she was doing, and she was choosing to do it with him.

In fact, she settled against him, her body pressing nicely against his. Still clasping the pins in his hand, he brought his arms around her and deepened the kiss. She wrapped her arms around his neck, seeming to melt in his embrace, something he rather liked. She was giving herself willingly to him, and he appreciated it.

He traced her lower lip with his tongue, and she parted her lips for him. Accepting her silent invitation, he interlaced his tongue with hers, savoring the taste of her. The kiss excited him to the point where he thought his heart might burst. He couldn't recall a time when he felt as if he was losing control of everything but knowing he was safe at the same time.

When their kiss ended, he continued to hold her. Her head settled on his shoulder and he kissed the top of her head, noting the sweet fragrance of her soap. "May I call you Claire?"

"You have been all along," she murmured.

"Yes, but I want to call you by your Christian name as a term of endearment from now on."

She nodded. "I'd like that. Can I call you by your Christian name?"

"Yes. It's Nathaniel, but I like to be called Nate."

"I like the name Nate. It suits you."

Smiling, he kissed the top of her head again. After a few moments passed, he reluctantly pulled away from her. "Are you ready to draw another picture?"

She nodded and retrieved her drawing pad and the flower. This time he watched her as she drew, and as much as he couldn't figure out what image she had in mind, he noted her intense focus as she worked. She might not have a talent for art, but he admired her dedication to doing her best.

When she was done, she positioned the pad so he got a good look at it. "What do you think it is?"

He honestly had no idea. It looked like a mix between a dog, a bunch of circles, and a portion of a house. He took a deep breath, and hoping not to upset her, ventured, "Is it a dog?"

She glanced down at her drawing. "A dog? How can you see a dog in this picture?"

So it wasn't a dog. He couldn't be surprised. The long nose might have belonged to a horse. It would also explain the partial house and circles.

Before he could guess it was a horse, she sighed and said, "It's you."

"Me?"

"I thought it'd be fun to try drawing you. I've never drawn a person before." Her disappointment gave way to a grin. "I told you I'm not good at drawing. I want to know how well you can draw, and for my part of telling you what to do, I want you to draw this." She handed him the pad and the wildflower.

"Wouldn't you rather have me kiss you?"

Her face grew pink. "Maybe next time, but I'm interested in what you can do."

Amused, he brought his attention back to the pad and looked at what was supposed to be his face. He rubbed his nose. It wasn't that big, was it?

She closed the space between them and all thoughts about how big she thought his nose was flew from his mind. Instead, he became aware of how nice she felt against him. Yes, sitting close like this was much better than sitting apart. Smiling, he went to a clean piece of paper and did his best to draw the flower. To his surprise, it didn't look too bad.

"You draw better than I do," she noted, a slight disappointment in her voice.

"If I can't be as pretty as you, I might as well draw better," he teased.

Her gaze met his and she laughed. Taking that as his cue, he wrapped her in his arms and kissed her once more, and as he expected, the rest of the world faded into the background once again.

Chapter Seventeen

The day had been such a pleasant one, and Claire hated to return to the house. Outside, while taking a pleasant stroll, noting the flowers, and drawing with her husband, it was easy to forget how tense things had been since she married him. This was a new side of him, one she hoped to see more often.

It wasn't that he'd been cruel to her before, but he hadn't taken the time to get to know her, to realize she wasn't the person he assumed her to be. And now he was taking that time, something that thrilled her to no end. If only the day would last forever.

After they ate dinner, they relaxed on the settee in the drawing room, enjoying a hot cup of tea. He sat close to her, something that made her heart flutter with nervous excitement. Though she sipped her drink, she hardly tasted the liquid.

Once he finished his tea, he leaned back and rubbed her back. "Tell me about yourself, Claire. What do you like? What do you not like? I already know you like to draw."

"Yes, you've seen me do my best, though no one would know it to look at it," she mused and sipped more of her tea.

He chuckled. "You draw fine."

"You're only saying that to be nice."

"I believe that, as your husband, I have a right to be nice when I look at your drawings."

"As long as you don't show them to anyone."

"If I told you I knew someone who could put one in a museum, would you be alarmed?"

She gave him a sharp look, knowing full well he'd have to be daft to consider such a thing, but then she caught the sparkle in his eye and realized he was teasing. Forcing back a grin, she admonished, "And to think Lord Clement accused you of not knowing how to tell a joke."

"You can't believe what he says. The poor man has this ridiculous notion that ladies run away from him whenever he's around. He seems to think he sprouted a second head instead of having a simple limp."

She giggled and put her cup on the tray. "That's not nice, Lord Roderick. He holds you in high esteem."

Slipping his arm around her waist, he drew her close to him and kissed her cheek. "You can't fault him for having good taste. He might not have told you this, but he wishes he was me."

Playfully swatting his arm, she laughed. "I didn't mean to imply he wants to be like you."

"He does. Even if he doesn't say it, he does. It's been like that ever since we were children. He spent his whole life living in my shadow, trying to be like me." He shrugged. "What am I supposed to do? Tell him the truth? That he's doomed to be second best?"

"You're a horrible friend," she teased.

He shot her a wicked grin. "No. I just want to be sure you don't think you married the wrong gentleman." After he kissed her, he added, "What I have to say is for your ears only. Don't go spreading it around."

Intrigued, she nodded.

"The truth is, I admire him. Despite what he thinks, he attracts people, even ladies, because of his natural enthusiasm for life. He's the kind of person people want to be friends with, and he always finds a positive way to look at things. And better yet, no matter what happens, he's there to lend a helping hand. Few gentlemen are better than him."

Touched, she smiled and snuggled against him. "That's a beautiful sentiment."

"Which is why you'll understand no one must ever know I said it."

"I'm sure he knows."

"Maybe."

"How did you two meet?"

"In school, I was quiet. I spent most of my time reading, and some of the children were giving me a hard time. Perry stood up for me." Giving her a wink, he added, "And he's been clinging to me ever since." He gave her a light squeeze. "What about you? What was it like for you while you were growing up?"

"Good. Even though I wasn't good at it, my favorite lessons were painting and drawing. Lilly preferred to play the piano, which she was good at. She still likes to play it from time to time, mostly when people come by to visit. I got along with others, but Lilly was my dearest friend."

He rubbed her back and smiled. "And your parents are staying in London until she finds a husband?"

"Yes. They're hoping they won't have to give her a third Season."

He finished drinking his tea and held onto the cup while studying her. "While we're in London, we'll have your family to our home for dinner. I should get to know them better, and it'd be good for you to see them before we return to Weston. We'll visit them after we return here, of course, but it won't be more than a couple times a year. But with any luck, you'll be preoccupied with a child soon enough, and you won't be bored anymore."

"I'm not bored now that you're here, but it'll be nice to have a child."

"I'd like to have a child, too." He brushed her cheek with his fingers, his touch making her skin tingle in delight. "Would it be forward of me to ask if I can come to your bedchamber tonight?"

Despite her apprehension about being in bed with him, she shyly said, "You can come to my room."

He lowered his head and kissed her, his lips soft and warm on hers. When he ended the kiss, he smiled at her. "Would you like to take another walk? We could watch the sunset."

"That'd be lovely."

He helped her stand up, and together, they left the drawing room to enjoy more time outside before it got dark.

***

It occurred to Nate that going to his wife's bedchamber that night might be rushing the newfound intimacy they'd found, but when he asked her if he could, she welcomed him. And after having read Lord Edon's book and spending the day kissing her, he didn't have the kind of restraint required to wait for another day before he asked to be with her in bed.

Before he went to her bedchamber, he took the time to slip into his nightclothes and, though he'd rather die than admit it, took out Lord Edon's book from his cabinet to review the section that explained, in surprising detail, how he could ease Claire into the consummation of their marriage.

When he was confident he could remember what to do and in what order he needed to do it, he closed the book and placed it back in the safe. Straightening up, he adjusted his robe and left his room. He could have used the door adjoining their rooms, but she wasn't expecting him from there and he didn't want to alarm her. So he went down the hallway and knocked on her door.

He expected her to call him in, but she opened the door, and this time there was no decanter full of sherry to get drunk from. She wore a long robe that covered her from her neck to her ankles, but even so, the candlelight revealed more details in her figure than her day clothes did. He took in the round curve of her breasts and nice shape of her hips. The fact that he was about to see her without her robe excited him to no end, but he refused to rush it. The book insisted he take things slowly.

As she closed the door, he cleared his throat. "Are you nervous?"

She offered a shy smile and nodded. "I know. It's silly. But being this is our first time, I don't know what to expect."

"You finally believe me when I said nothing happened on our wedding night?"

"If we had, you would have told me today while you were telling me everything else. I'm sorry I didn't believe you."

He reached for her hand and drew her close to him. "You have nothing to worry about. I won't do anything to hurt you."

She cleared her throat. "Should we go over to the bed or do we need to do something else first?"

He gave her a kiss. "Did you need to do anything? Like brushing your hair or some other thing ladies do before they go to sleep?"

Her eyebrows rose in amusement. "You came in here so we could go to sleep?"

Delighted she was quick on her feet with a clever response, he wrapped his arm around her shoulders and took her to the bed where the covers were pulled back. Though he sensed a slight unease in her movements, she slipped off her robe, and he was surprised she didn't wear anything underneath. Sure, when she was drunk, he understood why she removed everything in front of him. People did things they wouldn't normally do while drunk, but she did it while she wasn't drunk and that told him she trusted him, something he didn't take for granted.

170

Not knowing what else to do, he followed her lead and removed his robe and nightclothes. He slipped under the covers with her and drew her into his arms. Her flesh was soft and warm, her arms welcoming him as she embraced him. It seemed natural to start with a kiss, so lowered his head and brought his lips to hers. Despite her hesitation, she responded to him. In short time, he noticed her relax. Her muscles weren't as tense as before, and she was growing more responsive to his kiss.

He parted his lips, and this time, she followed suit, inviting him into her mouth. His tongue brushed her lips before he interlaced his tongue with hers. Kissing her was quickly becoming his favorite activity. He'd kissed her throughout the day, mindful to wait until they were alone before doing more. They'd spent the majority of the day either outside or in the drawing room which seemed to be her favorite places. And now as he was kissing her, the patience in their kisses from earlier was quickly giving way to the more insistent passions that had been lurking beneath the surface.

He became aware of her breasts which felt heavenly against his chest, the curve of her waist and hip as he ran his hand down her body, and the way her flesh cushioned his arousal. Recalling Lord Edon's book, he restrained his urge to rush things and slowed his exploration of her body. He brought his hand up her back and caressed her neck and shoulders to further relax her. It worked. She melted against him.

He ended the kiss and lowered his head so he could kiss her neck and ear. She let out a contented sigh and wiggled against him, signaling that she was enjoying what he was doing. Encouraged, he continued kissing her neck as his hand went from her shoulder to her breast. Excitement surged through him as he cupped her breast in his hand and brushed her nipple. She shivered so he did it again and was rewarded with a low moan.

Recalling the book he'd read, he spent considerable time touching and kissing her. He explored her entire body, running his hands along her arms, her breasts, her abdomen, her legs, and her feet. The book recommended avoiding the area between her legs until he'd massaged the other areas of her body, and he was determined to focus on doing everything the book said, even if a part of him was getting impatient.

From time to time as he ran his hands along her body, he'd glance at her face to judge how much pleasure she was deriving from what he was doing. While he didn't completely understand why her expression seemed to fluctuate from pleasure to pain, he was reassured that she was enjoying what he was doing by the way she gripped the bed sheets.

He turned his attention back to her legs, massaging her calves and then he rubbed her feet, trying to remember the areas that were best to focus on. When he knelt between her legs, he kissed the back of her knees and the inside of her thighs, all too aware of the woman's flesh that beckoned to him. At such close proximity, he couldn't resist the chance to study it, and he shifted so that he got a good view of her in the candlelight.

He unwittingly thought of the beauty she found in flowers, but he much preferred her body to them. Her scent and the way she looked and felt were much better. He thought to tell her this but decided he'd better not in case he distracted her. As it was, she was caught up in the moment, which was exactly where he wanted her.

He got up on his hands and knees and shifted so that he was next to her. He brought his lips to hers as his hand settled between her legs. She parted her legs for him, allowing him the chance to finally explore her as he'd been eager to do since he'd seen her naked on their wedding night. He brushed her entrance, taking note of her swollen flesh before he entered her, using one finger to detect how wet she was. To his satisfaction, she easily received him, her body pulling him in deeper. He slid in another finger and she moved her hips and groaned.

172

Ending their kiss, he kissed her neck and then traveled lower until his mouth was on the breast closest to him. He centered on her nipple and traced it with his tongue. She gasped and clutched his shoulders. Surprised that his tongue should elicit such a strong reaction, he traced her nipple again and was rewarded with an impatient groan.

His fingers continued to stroke her, and he slipped another finger in, this time noting the virginal part of her. He gently worked on stretching her out while he continued to tease her nipple. From her reaction, he thought teasing her nipple was a good way to distract her from his efforts on getting her ready for him.

When he realized she was as ready for him as she was going to get, he moved his thumb over her sensitive nub. The book said she'd be most likely to climax if he could stroke it long enough, and if she could climax, then she'd be further relaxed. He finally found it after what was beginning to seem like a futile search, not that she seemed to mind since she grew more vocal in expressing her pleasure. But it would have been embarrassing if he hadn't found it, so he was relieved when he did. It'd be best if she assumed he knew exactly what he was doing, after all.

He proceeded to rub her sensitive nub in circular motions, mindful to start slow and increase the pressure and speed. Her moans grew louder, and she murmured for him to keep going as her hips rocked in rhythm with his caress. He continued stroking her until she let out a sharp cry and stilled. Her hands tightened on his shoulders, and her flesh clasped around his fingers. Though he'd read about the female orgasm, he was still surprised by how satisfying it was to know he'd brought her to completion.

When she relaxed, he removed his fingers from her and shifted so that he was, once again, settled between her legs. He entered her and stilled, surprised she remained tight despite his efforts to avoid this. He studied her face and noticed her slight grimace. After a couple seconds, she moved her hips, giving him the silent assurance he needed in order to continue. The experience was more heavenly than he imagined. He moved inside her, aware of the way she clenched around him. She wrapped her legs around him, an action which served to pull him deeper into her. They worked together, and his thrusting increased until he couldn't hold back from the inevitable anymore and he released his seed. The moment seemed to be suspended in time as he savored the pleasure of finding fulfillment inside her.

He collapsed in her arms, out of breath and lightheaded. After a minute passed, he lifted his head and kissed her. "How do you feel?" he whispered, brushing back a strand of her hair from her cheek.

She smiled. "Wonderful."

Relieved, he returned her smile. "Good."

He kissed her again, this time letting his lips linger on hers. Afterwards, he settled next to her and gathered her into his arms. She let out a sigh of contentment. Pleased, he kissed the top of her head and fell asleep.

Chapter Eighteen

Three days later, Claire pulled aside the curtain in the drawing room. London looked much better when she wasn't miserable. It'd been a full day since she and Nate arrived in town, and the first thing she did was send a missive to her family. Now as she scanned the busy streets, she wondered how long it'd take to get their response.

Not seeing anyone walk up the front steps to deliver a letter, she let the curtain fall back into place and returned to the writing desk. She wasn't in the mood to draw or write, but she wasn't sure what else she could do. Nate went to White's to see if Perry was there so he could tell him about his ward.

She glanced at the blank paper in front of her. Maybe she could draw Weston. Even if it turned out to look like a lopsided rectangle with more lopsided shapes around it, at least she'd be drawing something she was interested in, even if no one else knew what it was.

Just as she picked up her graphite pencil, the door opened and the butler gave a bow. Thankful for the reprieve, she stood up and walked over to him.

"Lady Roderick, a Mister Morris has asked to speak with you."

"Mister Morris?" She hadn't seen him since the night of the ball. Curious as to why he'd come to see her, she nodded. "Bring him in."

The butler hastened to obey, and when he returned, a nervous Mister Morris entered the drawing room with him.

Mister Morris bowed, and she curtsied. "Forgive me, Lady Roderick," he began. "I saw your husband in town today and thought you might be here. I should have requested an invitation to meet with you, but…"

It dawned on her why he was urgent to talk to her. "There's no need to apologize, Mister Morris." Turning to the butler, she asked, "Will you bring us some tea?" As the butler left the room, she motioned to the chair. "Will you please sit?"

"Thank you, Lady Roderick," he replied.

She sat on the settee and waited for him to sit before she said, "I take it you heard about my sister and Lord Hedwrett."

"Yes. In fact, I wanted to seek your help. She didn't accept my proposal last year. I'm not foolish enough to believe she'll ever marry me. I have money but no title."

The butler entered the room and set the tray set on the table between them. After he left, she poured the tea in the cups and handed one to Mister Morris.

"What would you like me to do?" she asked as she picked up her cup.

"I thought you might talk to her. If she won't marry me, then so be it, but I want to see her married to a gentleman who'll be good to her."

"Exactly what do you want me to say?"

"I'm not sure. If I tell her Lord Hedwrett's been known for engaging in undesired behaviors, I think she'll assume I'm lying because I don't want to see her with another gentleman."

"Mister Morris, if I knew what those undesired behaviors were, I'd be in a better position to tell her to avoid him." Nate hadn't been forthcoming with the information, and while she appreciated the fact that he and Mister Morris wished to protect her from the more ungentlemanly actions of men, she didn't know how she could get her sister to take her seriously. When she saw the hesitation in his face, she added, "Do you want her to end up with Lord Hedwrett because I couldn't adequately explain how horrible he is for her?"

"You're right. As much as I hate to do it, it'd be worse to see her married to him." He took a deep breath. "Lord Hedwrett's passion is money. One of the most efficient ways he acquires it is to give out loans, and he's been known to charge up to thirty percent in interest. This often puts the person who took the loan at a disadvantage. If he can't pay the money, Lord Hedwrett's been known to take possession of valuable objects or require personal favors."

"Why would anyone ask him for a loan if he demands so much in interest?" she asked, baffled that anyone would agree to an outrageous interest rate of thirty percent.

"Desperate gentlemen do desperate things, and most don't read the contract before they sign it. Lord Hedwrett has been known to lie, and unless a gentleman is careful, he can get trapped."

Remembering the cup in her lap, she lifted it and drank some of the tea. She wasn't sure if she wanted to know more but ventured, "Is there anything else I should tell my sister about him?"

"He seeks alliances with those in influential positions and has been known to use people to accomplish those goals. And to put it delicately, there's nothing he won't do. He," he shifted uncomfortably in his chair and cleared his throat, "let a duke be with his sister in a compromising situation. I'm sorry, my lady, but I dare not say more than that. I wouldn't put it past him to use your sister in a similar fashion."

The color drained from her face. "I don't understand. Shouldn't gentlemen refuse to do business with him for his…actions?"

"He has money, influence, and he's discrete. Some of us are aware of what he does, but since he's careful to not do this in public, the ton can look the other way."

"I understand." She placed the cup on the tray, unable to finish any more tea. "I'll tell my sister next time I see her."

"Thank you," he replied, relaxing. "If your sister desires a titled gentleman, there are a couple who are unmarried and will treat her well. Lord Clement and Lord Lewis are admirable. Perhaps suggesting them will lead her in the right direction."

She sighed, wishing once again that her sister would take the time to understand how much he loved her. "I have the highest amount of respect for you, Mister Morris."

"Thank you." He rose to his feet and bowed. "I hope she'll listen to you."

She nodded, wondering if her sister would. If Lilly hadn't been so enamored with a gentleman's title, she could be very happy with Mister Morris. After he left the room, she spent a few minutes contemplating what she'd say to her sister before she got ready to leave the house. She didn't know if talking to her sister would do any good. Her sister hadn't made it a habit of listening to her before when it came to the affairs of the heart, but it was worth a chance. Knowing what she did about Lord Hedwrett, she'd always regret it if she didn't tell her sister everything she knew.

***

Nate found his friend at White's, reading a book. Stepping in front of him, Nate shook his head and clucked his tongue. "I can't believe what I'm seeing. I took your ward off your hands so you could spend time in London seeking a wife, and this is what I find you doing? If you were going to come to this establishment, the least you could do is talk to fathers who are eager to see their daughters married off."

Perry looked up from his book and chuckled. "You can't be upset with me for wanting to read a good book."

"I can when you have more important things to do." He sat next to him and checked the title of the book. "You're not even reading nonfiction."

"Not all reading has to be spent learning something, Nate." He closed the book and studied his friend. "Are you here to pay the rest of your steward's lenders?"

"I already paid them, but I just got a letter from Lord Hedwrett. He's demanding I see him again. He seems to think he wasn't properly paid."

"That's not surprising. He's known for demanding more from those who owe him money. Too bad your steward is in prison or else he could handle the ridiculous haggling process you're about to endure."

"If he thinks he's getting more money from me, he's sorely mistaken. He's fortunate I decided to make good on the debts."

Perry grinned. "I'm sure you'll put him in his place."

"I will. And after I do, I'll be free to spend more time with my wife." When Perry didn't respond, he turned his attention back to him and saw the bewildered expression on his face. Laughing, he added, "Yes, I've discovered that Lady Roderick isn't as bad as I feared."

"It took you two months of being at Weston to figure that out?"

"To be fair, I've had some accounts to settle. I wasn't there the entire time."

"I don't envy the work you had to go through. At least it's almost over." After a moment of silence, he drummed his fingers on the armrest and gave a tentative look in Nate's direction. "I almost hate to ask, but is my ward a responsible young gentleman yet?"

"Not yet, but I haven't given up hope."

"What did he do?"

"He convinced my wife to dress up as a stableboy so she could run off to London to visit her family."

"He didn't."

"He did. Fortunately, I caught her before she headed off to London by herself."

"Did anyone see her?"

"Just the butler and stable master, and I gave them a little financial incentive to keep the matter quiet."

"I'm sorry my ward is so difficult, Nate."

Nate grinned. "Don't be. He's cleaning chamber pots now."

His jaw dropped. "You didn't!"

"He'll continue doing that until he either learns how to be responsible or he no longer needs a guardian."

Perry winced but nodded. "I wouldn't have had the courage to do that to him, but I see the wisdom in your actions."

"You're much too nice, Perry. Your ward knew that and took advantage of it."

"I wish I could disagree with you, but I can't."

Shifting in his chair, Nate asked, "Did you pay any ladies a call while I was away?"

"A couple, but I don't think any were interested."

"Why not?"

He motioned to his cane.

Nate groaned and rolled his eyes. "You can't still be using that as an excuse."

"To be fair, you can't be using my time spent disciplining my ward as an excuse why I can't find a wife either."

"Your ward had a part of it, and I realize some ladies don't like the idea of marrying a gentleman with a cane. However, you're using both of those reasons as excuses for the real reason."

"And what is the real reason?"

"Maybe you worry she won't like you once she gets to know you. Maybe you don't think you have anything interesting to say."

Perry shrugged.

Recalling Perry's words to him a month earlier, he quipped, "I thought your advice was to pick a lady who was nice to look at instead of worrying about getting along with her."

Perry grinned. "No. That was my advice to you since you were sure that you'd never be happy as a married gentleman. Fortunately for you, marriage has been good to you. I can't recall the last time you smiled without being threatened to do it."

He motioned to the chessboard not too far from them. "Why don't we play a game?"

With a nod, Perry retrieved his cane and rose to his feet. "Losers before winners," he teased, gesturing for Nate to go first.

"Don't be so sure you'll win, Perry. I have a feeling your luck has taken a turn for the worse."

"We'll see about that."

Amused, Nate led the way to the chessboard.

***

Her parents' butler opened the door and greeted Claire with a smile. "Lady Roderick, it's a pleasure to see you doing so well."

"Thank you," she replied as she entered the townhouse.

She followed him into the drawing room, hardly believing she'd been staying in this townhouse just over two months ago. Back then, she'd felt a mixture of hope and apprehension at the task of finding a husband. Fortunately, things had turned out better than she'd hoped with Nate. With any luck, her sister would have a good marriage. She clenched her hands together and wondered if her sister would even listen to her.

She turned to face the door when she heard footsteps coming down the hallway. A smile crossed her face when she saw her parents.

"Claire, my dear," her father softly spoke, a warm smile on his face.

She hurried across the room so she could hug him and then her mother. "I missed you."

"We missed you, too," her mother whispered, holding her close. "But we're glad you married so well."

When she pulled away from her mother, she sighed. "Marriage is more than about having a gentleman with title and money."

"You misunderstand your mother," her father replied. "We can tell you're happy with your husband."

Her eyebrows furrowed. "You can?"

"Certainly," her mother said. "It's in your face. You're glowing."

"I knew Lord Roderick would be good to you," her father added with a wide smile. "A gentleman's reputation precedes him."

The butler came into the room with their tea.

"We should sit and talk," her father said, directing her to a chair.

Claire sat and waited for them to sit across from her. After she picked up her cup and drank some tea, she looked at the doorway. It wasn't unusual for her sister to take her time coming to the drawing room, but she should have been here by now. "Where's Lilly?"

Her mother glanced at her father. "She's at the museum with Lord Hedwrett. Your aunt agreed to act as chaperone."

"You don't sound happy about that," Claire noted, and though she was disappointed her sister wasn't there, she saw this as the perfect opportunity to learn what her parents thought about him.

Her father finished drinking his tea and set his cup on the tray which rested on the table between them. "We're not happy about it."

"Then why did you permit her to go with him to the museum?" she asked.

"You know Lilly's always been a willful girl. If I tell her she can't see him, she'd find a way to be with him. God forbid she should run off to Gretna Green. You know how stubborn she can be. She wants to do what she's been advised not to do. What your mother and I are hoping to do is help her find a more suitable match. I've invited a viscount over tomorrow. Perhaps she might find him to her liking."

Claire sipped her tea and studied her parents' expressions. "What about Mister Morris?"

"Mister Morris is a fine gentleman. He'd treat her well," her father said.

"He has no title," her mother commented. "Your father and I hoped you both would find husbands with a title."

"But is a title that important?" She took another sip from her tea before setting the cup down. Leaning forward, she continued, "To what extent does a title matter if she's with someone like Lord Hedwrett?"

"I understand what you're saying, Claire," her mother replied. "And I don't want her with Lord Hedwrett."

Claire shot her a pointed look, and her father rested his hand on her mother's arm. "Claire, titles are important. They are a legacy. Your firstborn son will one day be an earl. We wanted something similar for your sister. But," he squeezed her mother's arm, "a gentleman with money and no title who treats Lilly well is better than a titled gentleman who won't."

Her mother nodded. "Yes, I know, and you're right. However, she also wants to be with a titled gentleman. You know how she is, Claire. She wants the finer things in life and to be referred to as a lady. She refused Mister Morris' suit by choice.

Your father and I might have hoped you two would marry titled gentlemen, but she hopes for it, too."

"Yes, she does," she acknowledged. And that was the tricky part. It was what prevented Lilly from marrying Mister Morris last year. *Marriage isn't about love*, Lilly had told Claire. *It's about being practical and using wise judgment.* Except her sister wasn't showing wise judgment, and perhaps that was why she needed to warn her sister about the type of person Lord Hedwrett was. Maybe she would listen, given the facts. She rose to her feet. "I must return home. My husband will be due back soon, but before I leave, I hope you and Lilly will come to my home for dinner tomorrow."

They stood up, and her father nodded. "We'd be delighted."

After exchanging their good-byes, Claire left the house. She glanced back one time as she reached the carriage. Her parents smiled and waved from the doorway, and she returned the gesture before getting into her seat. As the coachman closed the carriage door, she took a good look at the townhouse they rented. It had to cost her father a pretty penny to linger in London in hopes of finding her sister well married. At least they all agreed Lord Hedwrett wasn't the right choice. She took comfort in knowing that they wouldn't agree to such a match, but she knew they were right. Her sister could be impulsive and headstrong when she wanted something badly enough. The problem was, how was she going to convince Lilly that she wanted Mister Morris more than a titled gentleman?

Chapter Nineteen

*W*hen Claire stepped through the entryway of her townhouse, she hardly had time to greet the butler when her gaze went to her husband who came out of the library and headed in her direction.

"I'm glad you're home," Nate said with an excited grin on his face.

Curious, she studied his expression. Most of the times she'd been around him, he'd been serious, almost to the point where she thought he'd suffer pain if he smiled. But ever since that day he'd found her in the stable, he'd done a complete turnaround. It was a very pleasant change, but it still took her by surprise. Perhaps in the months to come, he'd smile all the time and she would forget how serious he could be.

She waited for the butler to leave before she asked, "Is there something you want to tell me?"

"Yes, there is. You're beautiful."

Pleased, she blushed. "Thank you, my lord, but I thought something happened that prompted you to run over to greet me when I stepped through the door."

"Oh yes. There is. This evening, they're launching a balloon."

"A balloon?"

"Yes. I hear it's one of the bigger ones. It should be a sight to see. Will you go with me?"

"I didn't think you took delight in such leisurely pursuits."

He shrugged and grinned. "Maybe it's time I did."

"Maybe, and who knows what other fun things you might find to do now that you no longer have your nose stuck in one of those boring books in your library," she teased, unable to resist the urge to be playful.

"I feel it's fair to warn you that I'll never find those books boring, but I am finding you more interesting."

"I'll accept that."

Chuckling, he gave her a kiss. "Did you have a nice visit with your family?"

"Yes, but I just saw my parents. My sister was at the museum with Lord Hedwrett."

He grimaced.

If she wasn't aware of how horrible Lord Hedwrett was, she'd laugh because every time she said his name, Nate seemed to have an involuntary reaction to show his displeasure. "I'm worried she'll marry him," she softly confessed, not wishing for anyone to overhear her. "I want to talk to her, but I won't see her until tomorrow when my family comes over here for dinner."

He sighed and took her by the elbow so he could lead her to the drawing room. When he shut the door, he motioned for her to sit on the settee. After a moment's hesitation, she obeyed, wondering if there was something more dastardly she'd learn about Lord Hedwrett than what Mister Morris had told her. Her stomach tightened into a knot as he joined her.

He took her hands in his and gave her a sympathetic look. "Claire, I know how much you love your sister, but the problem is, you can't make her act in a certain way. I want to make sure if your sister marries him, you did everything you could to prevent it."

"I know I can't control what she does."

"But do you understand you shouldn't feel guilty about it?" He squeezed her hands and kissed her. "Be there for her and tell her what you have to but understand she has to make her own decisions, all right?"

She nodded.

A knocking at the door made her jump, and he chuckled. "It's all right. There are no ghosts in this house." He stood up and answered the door.

She released her breath and relaxed. From the other side of the door, she saw the butler hand Nate a missive. She resisted the urge to get up and find out who it was from. It wasn't her business unless he wanted her to know, and already, he'd told her more than most husbands probably told their wives. It meant he trusted her, and that made her want to love him all the more.

Nate closed the door and returned to her. "Lord Hedwrett says he'll meet with me next week at five."

"I thought you paid him off."

"I did, but he disagrees. Don't worry. The matter will be resolved soon enough. In the meantime, there's not much I can do but wait." He grinned. "I suppose that's not so bad. I'll be able to do your bidding."

Noting his playful tone, she smiled, feeling the heaviness of her sister's situation lift from her shoulders, even if it was for a while. "Then I insist on seeing that balloon launch you mentioned."

He gave her a kiss. "As you wish, but first, I believe it's time for dinner."

She giggled as he kissed her neck. "You don't seem to be interested in food."

"I will be," he murmured, his lips brushing against her ear. Lifting his head, he wrapped his arms around her. "In a moment."

His lips descended on hers, and she forgot all about eating.

***

It wasn't until after dinner the next day when Claire got a chance to talk to her sister. Since Claire asked to talk to Lilly in the drawing room, Nate took her parents to the library.

"All right. We're alone. What's so important that I can't play the piano right now?" Lilly asked as she ran her hand over the piano keys.

"Sit down," Claire suggested, patting the spot next to her on the settee.

Her eyebrows furrowed. "This must be serious."

"It is."

She hesitated for a minute but then joined Claire at the settee. "Why do I have a feeling I'm not going to like what you have to say?"

"You probably won't, but I want you to know that what I'm about to tell you, I tell you because I love you. You're more than my sister. You're my friend."

With a hesitant smile, she reached out to squeeze her hand. "You know I feel the same way about you. So what is this about? At dinner, your husband seemed friendly. Are you two still not getting along?"

"We are. Better than I hoped actually."

Her smile widened. "That's wonderful!"

"I want the same for you. Lilly, please don't marry Lord Hedwrett."

"Oh, that's what this is about. I suppose Mister Morris has come by to see you."

"And what if he did? He loves you."

"But he doesn't have a title. Claire, look at everything you have. You are *Lady* Roderick. Your husband owns this townhouse." She motioned to the room. "He doesn't rent it. I hear Weston is gorgeous. You have more rooms than you'll ever need. You have so many servants that you can't remember their names. You can buy as many gowns as you want whenever you want."

"No, I can't."

"I don't understand."

"You must swear that what I'm about to tell you, you won't tell anyone else."

Leaning forward, Lilly's eyes met her sister's. "Of course. You know I always keep your secrets."

Claire nodded. It was true. Lilly was good about that. After she took a deep breath, she lowered her voice. "My husband's steward was heavily in debt, and he stole money from the estate to compensate for it. Because of this, we have to be careful with what we buy until he can recover his financial standing."

Lilly's jaw dropped. "I had no idea…"

"No one did. These titled gentlemen don't go around advertising their lack of funds. There's no way to know."

"You think Lord Hedwrett might be in a similar predicament?"

"No. Lilly, that's not what I meant. I mean that I'm happy with my husband. He's a wonderful gentleman, and it doesn't matter to me that I can't buy new dresses for a while. That's the kind of marriage I want for you."

"And you don't think Lord Hedwrett will give me that?"

"No, I don't." She paused as she struggled to find a delicate way of telling her sister what Mister Morris told her. Fiddling with the skirt of her dress, she blurted out, "I heard Lord Hedwrett charges excessive interest on his loans and even allowed a gentleman of notable influence to ruin his sister." She held her breath and waited for her sister to respond.

Lilly frowned. "Did Mister Morris tell you this?"

"Yes, but—"

"How can you be sure Mister Morris isn't lying?"

"He's not the type to lie," Claire replied, surprised her sister would even accuse him of such a thing.

"I don't know. I think he might do anything to get me to marry him."

"But he does it out of love." When her sister sighed, Claire added, "And if it makes a difference, you'll be happy to know he told me he'll be happy to see you with a titled gentleman as long as he treats you well."

"I know his heart is in the right place."

"Don't you care about him?"

"I do."

"Then why not marry him?" Claire asked.

"He doesn't have a title, and a title is important."

Claire realized arguing with her sister wasn't going to do any good, but she had one option that might work if she was careful. Inspired, she glanced at the paper on her desk. "Lilly, will you do something for me, even if it's something foolish?"

Lilly's eyebrows furrowed. "I have to hear what you have in mind before I agree to it."

"I can't go into detail, but I want you to see what Lord Hedwrett is like when he doesn't know you're around."

"And how do you suggest we do that?"

Claire's lips curled up into a smile. "You leave that to me."

"You aren't thinking of doing something inappropriate, are you?"

"No more inappropriate than what you and our father did that night you two trapped me into marriage with Nate."

"Oh, you can't still be angry about that. Look at how well things turned out."

"Which is why I need to arrange for us to sneak into Lord Hedwrett's home. You'll see what I mean when the time comes. In the meantime, I need to write a letter to someone." Claire stood up and hurried over to her desk before Lilly could argue her way out of it.

Lilly rose to her feet but remained at the settee. "Who are you writing to?"

"Someone who's perfect for what I have in mind. Don't ask me anything else."

Though she gave her a cautious look, she crossed her arms and remained quiet as Claire finished writing the letter to Mister Robinson. If there was anyone who didn't care enough about propriety to help her, it was him. There was no way her husband would allow it if he knew, which was why she decided no one, not even Lilly, had to know until the time came for her to act on her plan. Once she sealed the letter, she gave it to the butler with orders to send it to Weston.

Afterwards, she and Lilly headed for the library, and when she opened the door, she was both delighted and surprised to see that Nate and her father were laughing at something they were reading in a book. Her mother looked over at her from where she stood with Nate and her father.

With a relieved smile, she hurried over to them. "I'm glad you're here," she told her daughters with a chuckle. "It's nice to see Lord Roderick and your father getting along so well, but I couldn't care less about political strategies."

"Are you saying my husband is boring?" Claire teased.

"I'm saying political discussions are boring," she clarified with a twinkle in her eye.

"Then we need to talk them into doing something interesting," Lilly said. "We could do charades."

"Yes, that's an excellent choice," her mother said excitedly. "I'll mention it to the gentlemen."

As her mother headed over to them, Claire gave Lilly a knowing look. "I was wondering when you'd suggest we play charades."

"It makes her happy. The least we can do is play the game," Lilly mused.

Grinning, Claire and Lilly joined her mother.

Chapter Twenty

One day before Nate was supposed to see Lord Hedwrett to settle the debt, Claire was beginning to despair that Mister Robinson wasn't going to send the clothes. But around noon, the butler informed her that a gentleman insisted on giving her a package in person. Relieved, she put aside her graphite pencil and paper and rose from her desk.

"Let him in," she told the butler.

As she walked over to the settee, the butler brought the young gentleman in, and she noticed the package he held under his arm. Good. Mister Robinson came through after all!

She waited until the butler left before she turned her attention to the gentleman who'd delivered the package. In a low voice, she said, "I'll pay you for the delivery."

Before she could go to her desk, the gentleman removed his mustache, hat and wig. "The clothes will only get you so far."

Her eyes grew wide. "Mister Robinson!" she hissed. "What are you doing here?"

"You'll need to sneak into Lord Hedwrett's house, and I don't think you and Miss Lowell are familiar with doing that."

"Granted, we aren't, but couldn't you have written instructions instead of coming in person?"

Looking amused, he shook his head. "Lady Roderick, this is something I can't explain. I have to show you how to do it.

I've been thinking about where we went wrong when you dressed up as a stableboy."

"I know what went wrong. My husband showed up."

"And he saw right away you were his wife. What you needed was a beard to help hide your face."

"You could have sent me a beard instead of delivering it in person."

"Ah, but have you ever snuck into a house as a chambermaid?"

She blinked, wondering what he was getting at. "Chambermaid? I thought we were talking about dressing up as men."

"No. That's too obvious. You and Lilly need to be chambermaids. I've been cleaning out chamber pots for a while now, and I've learned a couple of things. Not only is it the most disgusting job a person can have, but chambermaids are never seen or heard. It's the perfect way to hide. No one pays attention to them, but chambermaids pick up on everything everyone else is doing. That's the beauty of you and your sisters dressing up as chambermaids."

She wasn't sure about his plan, but as she thought about it, it had more appeal than dressing up as a stableboy again. "So you brought chambermaid clothes?"

"And wigs. This will work."

"You're not dressing up as a chambermaid, are you?"

He gasped and then laughed. "No. I will be a stableboy."

"It seems that you've thought of everything."

"I have."

"But what about my husband? You're supposed to be at Weston. He won't be happy to learn you're in London."

"I already took care of that. I wrote to Lord Clement and told him everything."

Her jaw dropped. "You didn't!" she hissed, glancing at the doorway to make sure no one was passing by. It was only by luck Mister Robinson chose to come by when her husband was at White's. If Nate had been there when Mister Robinson showed up... She'd rather not think of the implications of that one.

"I had to get his permission to leave Weston so Lord Roderick would agree to it. It worked. Lord Clement told your husband that he's not feeling well and needs me to tend to him for a few days. Then I'll return back to prison."

Despite her best intentions, she giggled. "Mister Robinson, you wouldn't be confined to a prison if you would behave like a gentleman. It's your own doing you're stuck cleaning chamber pots."

"Yes. I suppose you're right."

"I don't know what you were doing to get in trouble, but Lord Clement wouldn't have sent you to Weston to be under Lord Roderick's supervision unless he cared enough about you to prevent you from becoming as unsavory as Lord Hedwrett. Are you aware of his reputation?"

"Yes, but I don't do the things Lord Hedwrett does."

"Did Lord Hedwrett start out doing the things he does now? From what I understand, it was a progression. He pressed boundaries of acceptable behavior, and the more he got away with, the more boundaries he wanted to push. That's the problem with doing the wrong things. You're never satisfied. At some point, the misbehavior loses its thrill, and you need to seek out something that pushes more boundaries."

She heard footsteps approaching, so she motioned for him to put his wig, hat, and beard back on. He did and set the package down on her desk.

The butler carried the tea into the room and set the tray on the table. "Is there anything else you need, my lady?"

"No, thank you." She waited until he left before motioning for Mister Robinson to sit down. "While you're here, tell me how we can sneak into Lord Hedwrett's home tomorrow evening."

With a nod, he sat across from her in a chair and told her his plan.

***

"Claire, this is the most ridiculous thing you've ever done, and what's worse is that you're dragging me into it," Lilly said.

Claire adjusted her blond wig before putting on her maid hat. "I'm doing this because I love you, and after tonight, you'll be thanking me."

"If you say so." She adjusted her heavy skirt and sighed. "I can't believe chambermaids wear these clothes all the time. How do they manage?"

"They're probably used to it."

"Probably." She tucked some red strands of her wig under her hat and glanced at Claire. "How do I look?"

"Almost perfect." Claire walked over to her and added a fake beauty mark to her cheek. "There. Now it's perfect."

Though she sighed, there was a hint of amusement on her lips. "If I had known you had this sneaky side to you sooner, we could have done many fun things together."

"I thought we had fun while we were growing up."

"We did, but I had no idea you could be mischievous."

Claire decided she didn't want to know the type of mischievous activities her sister might do without her knowledge. What she was doing tonight was for a good cause. She motioned for Lilly to follow her to the door of her bedchamber. Thankfully, Marion hadn't checked on them. So far, they had gone undetected. All they needed to do was slip out the back and meet Mister Robinson down the street.

Claire took a deep breath to steady her nerves. This was her second time dressing up in a disguise, but this wasn't any easier than the first time. There was no doubt about it. Lilly had her pegged as someone who didn't want to act inappropriately, and she was right. This was making Claire break into a sweat. Taking a deep breath, she slowly opened the door and peered into the hallway. It was empty. Good.

She motioned to Lilly to follow her down the hall and noted that Lilly stood on her tiptoes and hurried after her, pretending to be anxious as she did so. Claire resisted the urge to roll her eyes. Leave it to Lilly to make fun of her.

Once they reached the servants' staircase, they snuck down the steps. Claire's heart pounded furiously in her chest, and she stopped at every sound. At what was her tenth time pausing to determine if someone was coming up the stairs, Lilly let out a loud sigh and pushed past her.

"We'll grow old and grey by the time we reach the bottom of the stairs at the rate you're going," Lilly whispered.

"I'm sorry. It's just that my husband would be upset if he found out I dressed up as a chambermaid and snuck into Lord Hedwrett's home."

She rolled her eyes. "This was your idea."

"I know that." And it would be worth it, even if Nate did find out.

Lilly lifted her skirts and bounced down the steps, not seeming to notice the noise she made. It was on the tip of Claire's tongue to warn her to be quiet, but she realized Lilly was too far ahead of her so she ran after her. Once they reached the bottom of the steps, they glanced at the kitchen where the kitchen maid was putting dishes away on the shelves. Since she had her back turned to them, they hurried to the back door and slipped outside.

Claire closed the door softly behind them and collapsed against it. They made it out of the house. Meeting Mister Robinson would be the easy part. Feeling much better, Claire joined Lilly and headed down the street.

"I don't know how you can be so calm," Claire softly said, not wishing for anyone to overhear.

As far as she could tell, the few people they passed didn't pay them any mind. Even so, she lowered her head whenever they walked by someone, but Lilly refused to bow her head. Was it possible Lilly was daring someone to discover who she was? It wasn't like it was dark out. The sun wouldn't set for another hour.

"No one cares who we are because we're supposed to be chambermaids," Lilly whispered. "You have nothing to worry about. Mister Robinson had a good idea."

Feeling better, Claire lifted her head. "You're right."

When they turned down the street where Lord Hedwrett lived, Claire spotted Mister Robinson wearing the same disguise he'd had on the previous day. Thankfully, he'd thought of how they would get into Lord Hedwrett's residence.

When they reached the youth, Claire asked, "Is my husband here?"

"He just got here. We'll go in through the back," he replied and turned to lead them around to the back of the residence.

"Aren't you afraid someone's going to see us?" Claire wondered, glancing behind them. So far, it looked like they remained undetected. With any luck, it would stay that way.

"I know the brother of Lord Hedwrett's butler's cousin. He assured me that the staff wouldn't notice me."

"What about us?"

"Oh, I gave you wigs and clothes so you'd look just like the chambermaids who work for Lord Hedwrett. You both don't look exactly like them, but as long as you don't make eye contact with anyone, they'll assume you're them."

"You thought through everything, didn't you?" Lilly commented, sounding impressed.

"You have to if you're going to get past Lord Roderick," he muttered. They reached the back door, and he glanced at Claire. "It's a good thing chambermaids aren't seen or heard."

198

Deciding not to comment, Claire waited for him to open the door and led Lilly into the house before she followed behind them. She shut the door behind her and hastened after them as they made their way to the servants' stairs. She noticed the butler collect a decanter and a couple of glasses to put on a tray. The butler looked in their direction but turned his attention swiftly back to the tray as if he hadn't seen them. She shook her head. Just how many connections did Mister Robinson have? There was no doubt about it. He had to be one of the most resourceful people she'd ever met.

They went up the stairs and down a hall, back down another flight of stairs and then back up. On their way through another hallway, she stopped him.

"Where are we going?" she whispered, though there was no one from the household in sight.

"We're going to the drawing room," he replied.

"But isn't it close to the entrance of this house?"

"Of course."

She forced back her exasperation. "Then why are we going up and down stairs as if we were going through a maze?"

"There's no point in sneaking into a house if you take the direct route."

At that, Lilly giggled.

Claire groaned. Leave it to her sister and Mister Robinson to think the unnecessary steps was funny. "Mister Robinson, the future of my sister's happiness is at stake."

He shook his head as if he couldn't believe what he was hearing. "Lord Hedwrett's brother told me he never starts with business. He likes to play a couple of games first. Right now your husband is probably trying to avoid playing for money. Lord Hedwrett has a tendency to cheat, too, so gentlemen have to be careful."

"I doubt Lord Roderick will be taken in by Lord Hedwrett's ploy."

"I have no doubt you're right, but that won't stop Lord Hedwrett from trying."

Claire glanced at Lilly, wondering what she thought of that, but Lilly was peering into one of the bedrooms. She went over to her and took her by the arm. "Come on, Lilly. We aren't here to see the house."

"But it's a beautiful one!" Lilly whispered. "The curtains are such a lovely shade of purple."

"Let's go," she muttered, dragging Lilly with her as Mister Robinson turned down the hallway so they could go down another flight of steps.

This time, he led them straight to the drawing room which was next to the saloon. To her surprise, he moved aside a portrait from the wall and motioned to a peephole in the wall. Her jaw dropped. What was the peephole doing there? Did Lord Hedwrett know it existed? Were there similar holes in her townhouse or at Weston? She'd have to inspect the rooms of her homes at her earliest convenience. In the meantime, she had more important things to think about.

She peered through the hole and saw Lord Hedwrett and her husband playing cards at a small round table. She backed away from the wall and gestured for her sister to look through it. As much as she wanted to watch what happened, it was more important Lilly got to see it instead. While Lilly looked through the peephole, Claire brought her ear to the wall. Though the words were mostly muffled, she was able to make out some of what they said. She furrowed her eyebrows and focused on what they were saying.

Chapter Twenty-One

"*A*re you sure you don't want to make the game more interesting by adding some money to the table?" Hedwrett asked, leaning forward in his chair.

"No," Nate said, wishing they could be done playing cards so they could get down to business.

He'd heard Hedwrett liked to wiggle as much money from others as possible, so Hedwrett's insistence that they play piquet hadn't come as a surprise, but he sure did wish he could tell Hedwrett what he could do with his greedy claws. But he couldn't. Instead, he had to hope that one of them would get a hundred points and end the game.

"Not much of a gambling gentleman, hmm?" Hedwrett shuffled the cards, and though Nate couldn't be sure, he thought he saw the gentleman slip a card under his sleeve. "I can't resist a challenge. Of course, I hear Lord Edon can bluff his way through any game."

"Oh?"

"You're in White's, aren't you?"

Nate nodded, not sure if he wanted to find out where this conversation was going.

"I haven't been there. I prefer Brooks's."

"Both are fine clubs," he cautiously said as Hedwrett dealt the cards.

"Lord Edon often plays games at White's, doesn't he?"

"Yes." He picked up his cards and glanced at them before he glanced at Hedwrett, wondering when, or if, he'd pull out the card he had slipped under his sleeve. "I can't stay here much longer. I have pressing matters to tend to at home." Sure, the pressing matters he referred to had to do with spending time with Claire, but he figured there was no need to explain what he meant to Hedwrett.

"I heard you're a gentleman who works hard, but it's never a bad idea to allow for some play."

Hedwrett wiggled his finger and clucked his tongue in a way that only served to annoy Nate further. For goodness' sake! Did Hedwrett think he was a child?

The door opened, and Nate glanced over to see the butler carrying a tray with a decanter and glasses on it. He shifted uncomfortably in the chair. He didn't mind drinking port wine, but he hoped Hedwrett wouldn't pester him to drink more than he usually did. As it was, the gentleman had managed to get him to play cards, and unlike other gentlemen, he hated to play cards. Nate bit back the urge to sigh in case Hedwrett realized how much he was bothering him.

"Do you collect wine, Lord Roderick?" Hedwrett asked as the butler poured some of it into their glasses.

"No, I don't, but my brother did."

"A shame. I make it a habit of only getting the best, and he was bragging he had some that dated back a century."

He exchanged a card from the deck stacked at the center of the table and studied it, trying to determine if he could use it to his advantage or if he should intentionally let the other gentleman win. "Not anymore. My brother got rid of them."

"I suppose he got tired of his collection." Picking up his glass, he drank almost the entire glass before setting it on the table and gave a satisfied smile. "No, this is not one of my vintage bottles, but I'm happy to say that it came from the Duke of Watkins. He knows a gentleman who can make wine that tastes as if it's been sitting in a bottle for a hundred years. I don't know what his secret is, but I wouldn't mind teaching it to my staff. God knows they could use something more to occupy their time. The other day, I caught the valet in a rather embarrassing situation with a chambermaid. Granted, these things happen, but if they insist on it, I'd rather they do it when there isn't work to be done." Hedwrett picked up a new card from the deck and looked at Nate's glass. "I hope you'll taste it."

After he picked up another card, Nate dutifully retrieved his glass and sipped the wine in it. How he wished he could leave already. The last thing he wanted was to hear Hedwrett gossip about his household.

"What do you think?" Hedwrett asked.

"About what?"

"The wine, of course."

"Oh!" Nate took another sip and nodded. "It's good." At least as good as any other wine he'd had. He didn't know what made it special, but he supposed taste was subjective.

"It's good, he says." With an exaggerated eye roll, he chuckled. "I hate to say this, Lord Roderick, but you don't know good wine if all you can say is that this wine is good."

Nate shrugged. "I'm preoccupied with the game. Shall we get back to it?" He lifted his cards, praying this would be the last round he'd have to suffer through.

"Yes. You're very focused."

"It's how I managed to rectify the damage my steward did."

Hedwrett smirked. "I suppose it is. Too bad we can't combine your steward's amiability with your ability to properly settle financial matters." He picked up another card, and with a wide smile, added, "I believe I got a hundred points, Lord Roderick."

Relieved, he set his cards down. Good. The game was finally over! Maybe now he could pay Hedwrett and go home.

"You're a terrible card player. No wonder you don't want to bet with money." Hedwrett let out a hearty laugh and motioned for the butler to pour him more wine. "Drink up, my lord. It's impolite to not accept my gift to you."

Nate picked up his full glass and forced himself to drink the wine. When he was done, Hedwrett motioned to the butler to pour more wine into Nate's glass, and as much as he wanted to protest, he didn't dare.

Hedwrett sat back in his large chair and sipped his wine. "You may leave," he told his butler with a dismissive wave of his hand. "Good help is so hard to find, don't you agree, Lord Roderick? Even this butler can't seem to remember where the good wine is located in my cellar. If I didn't know better, I'd say he was smuggling the good bottles to his room."

He let out another boisterous laugh. Nate glanced at the butler who closed the door behind him on the way out. No wonder Hedwrett's servants were known for either gossiping about him or running off as soon as they could. Hedwrett had no sense of diplomacy.

After Hedwrett drank half the contents in his glass, he let out a contented sigh. "Yes, that wine gets better every time I taste it. But never mind that. You have some money to give me. I won't take up any more of your time. I don't want to keep you away from those pressing matters at Weston."

Nate jumped up and followed Hedwrett to his desk where he pulled out his ledger and ran his fingers down one of the columns. "I'm afraid your ledger is incorrect. I don't owe you any more money."

"Why not?"

"Because I paid everything my steward owed you."

Hedwrett shrugged. "But there's still the matter of interest for being late."

"I came here to tell you I'm not paying it."

Hedwrett frowned. "I see you a week before making good on the debt. As far as I'm concerned, you owe me compensation for waiting."

Irritated, Nate placed his hands on the table and made eye contact with him. "I don't owe you anything."

"Is it because you don't have any more money? Did your steward leave you destitute?"

"My financial affairs are not your concern."

"Since you owe me some money, they are my concern, but I think I misjudged how much your steward foolishly wasted. Lord Roderick, I'm a reasonable gentleman. I'm sure we can come to an agreement. Perhaps if you'd allow me some time alone with your wife, we could let the extra interest go."

Nate didn't have time to think. He grabbed Hedwrett by the cravat and pulled him over the desk so their noses were barely touching. "If you ever make a suggestion like that to me again, I'll call you out to a duel, whether it's legal or not. That money I already gave you settles the debt, but if you feel inclined to press me further, I'll be sure to approach the gentleman you swindled the next time I'm at White's club. Do you understand?"

Hedwrett's eyes grew wide and he gulped, his face pale.

"Signal that you understand."

He nodded.

Nate released him. "You disgust me, Lord Hedwrett. If you come near me or my wife, I won't be responsible for what I do to you." He straightened up and exhaled to calm his nerves. "The account is settled. You won't be telling anyone otherwise."

Hedwrett reached for the bell at the corner of his desk and rang it. The door to the room opened. "Make sure Lord Roderick is escorted to his carriage," he told the butler, his voice a bit shaky.

Satisfied, Nate spun on his heel and headed out of the room.

***

"We have to get out of here," Mister Robinson whispered.

Claire and Lilly stepped away from the wall while he put the picture back in place. They hurried after him as he went to the door. He pressed his fingers to his lips and listened at the door as the butler led Nate out the front door. Claire dared a glance at her sister, wondering if she was as shocked by what Lord Hedwrett had said as she was. Lilly's face was pale, but she gave no indication as to what she was thinking. It was just as well. She'd have to talk to her sister later.

She turned her attention back to Mister Robinson. Once everything was quiet, he opened the door a crack. He nodded to them and led the way out the door and down a hallway until they reached the servants' steps. Once they were outside, she released her breath and followed Mister Robinson and her sister as they made their way around the side of the house.

To her surprise, Nate was talking to his footman. Claire paused for a moment, wondering why he wasn't already on his way to the house. Nate looked in her direction, and when his gaze met hers, his eyes grew wide. Gasping, she turned around and followed after Mister Robinson and her sister who had stopped a block away to wait for her.

As soon as she reached them, her sister asked, "Why did you stop?"

Keeping pace with her companions, Claire groaned. "I didn't expect my husband to still be in front of the house. It took me by surprise." She winced. "I think he knows it was me."

"You can't know that for sure," Mister Robinson said.

"Oh, but I can. He gave me the same look he did that day when he caught me dressed up as a stableboy."

Lilly halted her steps, grabbed Claire's arm, and turned her so they were facing each other. "You dressed up as a stableboy?"

She glanced behind her to make sure Nate's carriage wasn't coming down the street. "To see our parents, but mostly to see you."

"To see me?"

"Because you said Lord Hedwrett had taken an interest in you, and I wanted you to marry Mister Morris."

"Ladies, can you discuss this later?" Mister Robinson interrupted them.

Claire glanced to where he was pointing and saw Nate's carriage heading their way. Startled, she and the others hurried down the street.

"You don't have to worry about me," her sister told her. "I won't have anything else to do with Lord Hedwrett."

She breathed a sigh of relief. Once she reached her townhouse, Mister Robinson darted down another street, and Claire urged her sister into the house where they snuck up the servants' stairs and to her bedchamber.

In all her life, Claire had no idea she could change clothes as fast as she did, and afterwards, she stuffed the chambermaids' clothes and wigs into a trunk and slammed the lid. Out of breath, she motioned for Lilly to hurry to the drawing room. Once downstairs, they passed a surprised butler and made it to the room just in time for the front door to open.

Gasping, Claire sat down and struggled to slow her breathing. Lilly sat beside her, also out of breath. Nate was talking to the butler, and she decided that was her cue. She laughed, making sure it was loud enough for him to hear, and said, "Oh Lilly! You say the funniest things!"

To Lilly's credit, she joined her and laughed, too.

Nate entered the room, and she studied his face to judge whether or not he knew it'd been her dressed as a chambermaid outside Lord Hedwrett's house, but he gave no indication if he knew.

"Miss Lowell, it's a pleasure to see you again," he said with a bow.

Claire and Lilly stood, and Lilly curtsied. "It's a pleasure to see you as well, my lord." She turned to Claire and clasped her hands. "Thank you for everything. I must leave."

Claire smiled. "Thank you for coming."

"My coachman will take you home," Nate said.

Thanking him, Lilly left the room.

After a few moments of awkward silence, he walked over to Claire and kissed her. "Did you have a good visit with your sister?"

Unsure of how to best proceed, she cleared her throat and nodded. "It was very enlightening."

"I'm sure it was."

She bit her lower lip, wondering if he was going to mention Lord Hedwrett.

"Lady Roderick, the strangest thing happened tonight," he said.

Her eyebrows rose. "Oh?"

"Yes, there was this person who reminded me of you. I saw her just as I was leaving Lord Hedwrett's residence."

Blast it all! He knew! Just like last time, he was letting her know it right away, too. She got ready to defend herself when it occurred to her that someone might be watching them. "Wait a moment. I'll explain everything soon."

Without waiting for him to ask what she was doing, she hurried out of the room and checked to make sure there weren't any holes behind any of the paintings adjoining the drawing room. When she was assured that no one could spy on her and her husband, she returned to the drawing room. She shut the door and faced him. "I can explain."

Though he looked curious about why she left the room, he focused on her. "All right. I'm listening."

Good. It was a start. At least he wasn't judging her…yet. She went over to the settee and patted the space next to her. "Will you sit with me?" She expected him to insist he'd remain standing, but he complied and settled next to her. Good. That was definitely a good sign. "I wanted to show my sister that Lord Hedwrett wouldn't make a suitable husband, so I thought it'd be to her benefit to see him as he really is. The only way I could do that was to convince Mister Robinson to lend us some clothes—"

"Mister Robinson?"

She stared at his incredulous expression for a few seconds before she nodded. "Yes. Lord Clement's ward. So I wrote him a letter and asked—"

"You contacted Mister Robinson? The one who is supposed to be at Weston emptying chamber pots so he could learn responsibility?"

"To be fair, he did this as a favor to me, and he notified Lord Clement what he was doing and why. I think that was responsible of him, don't you?"

Though he looked uncertain, he said, "I suppose."

"So I asked him to bring me and Lilly a disguise. My plan was to sneak into Lord Hedwrett's townhouse so we could overhear you and him tonight. I thought perhaps he'd let something unpleasant slip in his conversation with you since gentlemen are more apt to be bold in their speech when ladies aren't around."

"You snuck into his house?"

"Yes."

"Did anyone see you?"

"His butler." When she saw his face fill with dread, she quickly added, "But his butler knows someone who is a relative of someone who knows Mister Robinson…or something to that effect."

He blinked and shook his head. "What?"

"Never mind. That part doesn't matter. What matters is that the butler was more than willing to turn the other way."

"The butler could tell Lord Hedwrett."

"He won't."

"How can you be sure?"

She shrugged. "I believe Mister Robinson when he said the butler could be trusted."

His eyes went heavenward and he let out a long sigh.

"Regardless, the matter is done now, and the important thing is my sister heard the conversation you and Lord Hedwrett shared."

His gaze returned to her and he grimaced.

"Yes, I heard everything, and Nate," she added as she snuggled up to him, "I think it's wonderful you stood up for me like that. It's nice to know you care about me."

His face softened and he smiled. "Of course, I care about you. You're more than my wife. You're my friend, and I love you."

Thrilled, she smiled in return. "I love you, too."

"But I don't like the way you're dressing up in disguises and sneaking off to places you shouldn't be. What if you get hurt? What if Lord Hedwrett had caught you and your sister? You might not always be lucky."

"I know. I won't do it anymore. I wouldn't have done it this time if I wasn't worried about my sister."

"You can come to me instead of Lord Clement's ward."

Her eyebrows rose in disbelief. "Can I?"

He started to answer her but hesitated. "I would have found a different way of handling things with your sister, but yes, I would have helped you."

Pleased, she kissed him. "In the future, I'll ask you to get me a disguise."

Though he sighed, she noted the amusement in his tone. "I have a feeling that being married to you will never be boring."

"I should hope not." Grinning, he pulled her to him, but before he kissed her, she asked, "Do you really know a gentleman at White's Lord Hedwrett swindled?"

"I'll tell you, but you must never tell anyone else, not even your sister."

She nodded her agreement.

"I was bluffing. I don't have any idea who he cheated."

"I have a feeling you do a better job of deceiving people than I do."

"I really hope you don't make it a habit of putting on disguises."

"I won't," she promised. Then with a wicked grin, she added, "Unless you want me to."

He chuckled and kissed her. She wrapped her arms around his neck and gave into the thrill of being with him. He deepened the kiss, and she parted her lips so his tongue could interlace with hers. At the moment, it was just the two of them, and as they continued to kiss, she became aware of the ache forming between her legs. Making love to him was still new, but she was quickly learning what brought her the greatest amount of pleasure. What she wanted to do was learn how she could best please him.

When their kiss ended, she pulled far enough away from him so she could make eye contact with him. "What can I do to please you?"

"You are pleasing me." He took her hand in his and kissed her palm, an action that caused delightful chills to run straight to her toes.

As he kissed her hand again, her gaze lowered to his pants, noting the outline of his erection. She'd seen him naked, but she hadn't gotten up the nerve to explore him. She wondered if she should now. He brought his mouth back to hers, his lips more demanding than before, evidence of his building passion.

"Nate," she whispered.

"Hmm?" he asked as he kissed her jawline and then her neck.

She sighed and leaned into him. This was one of the things that pleased her most. He brought his hand to one of her breasts and cupped it in his hand. His thumb brushed the area where her nipple was, and she involuntarily shuddered. She wanted to feel his bare hands on her flesh, but first, she wanted to explore him, to fully learn his body.

"Nate," she ventured again, her heart racing at the thought of even asking the question.

"What?"

His breath tickled her ear so she giggled. Thankfully, the simple action helped to ease her apprehension. She cleared her throat. "Can I...? That is, I haven't touched you everywhere yet."

He stopped kissing her and looked at her. "You want to know me better?"

That wasn't exactly the way she would have worded it, but the meaning was the same so she nodded despite her warm cheeks. He released his hold on her and removed his clothes. Her heart raced in anticipation. She wondered if he was nervous, but if he was, he didn't show it.

He offered a reassuring smile and brought her hands to his chest. "You can touch me anywhere you want."

Then he closed his eyes, something she appreciated since she felt awkward enough as it was without him watching her. Despite the warmth rising to her cheeks, she explored his chest, her fingers brushing the fine hairs and teasing his nipples which grew hard in response. He relaxed into the settee and ran his hand along her arm, a silent encouragement for her to continue. Her gaze went to his arousal and then to his eyes to make sure he hadn't opened them.

He still had them closed. Relieved, she lowered her hands, intrigued to find out what he'd feel like in her hands. He'd been inside her, something that brought her much pleasure. Now as she traced his erection, she tried to memorize every part of it. She lightly touched the tip and ran her fingers down his shaft. Tentatively, she wrapped her hand around him and lightly squeezed him. It struck her a strange thing that his skin was silky while he was hard. His hand clasped around hers. Surprised, she looked back at his face, but he still had his eyes closed.

"You can use more pressure," he whispered and tightened his hand so she squeezed him.

"What else do you like?" she softly asked, almost hesitant since it was a bold move on her part.

He brought her hand to the base of his shaft and then brought it swiftly up to his tip and then brought it back down again. He repeated the process several times until she got the hang of it. When he released her hand, she continued the action. It seemed such a wicked thing to do—touching a gentleman's naked body while she was fully dressed. But he moaned his appreciation and wiggled beneath her in a way that emboldened her to kneel in front of him so she could take him into her mouth.

He gasped in pleasure as she traced his tip with her tongue, tasting the salty bead of moisture along his slit. She took more of him into her mouth and sucked lightly while using her hand to squeeze the base of his shaft. He murmured his appreciation and cupped her face in his hands so he could guide her mouth up and down his shaft.

She followed his lead, aware of how this intimate contact was making her body ready for his entry. It also gave her a feeling of power to know she could make him moan and squirm in pleasure. She experimented to find out if he preferred it when she was going slow or fast, so she alternated between the two.

When she was satisfied with her exploration, he ordered her to sit on the settee. Highly aroused from being so intimate with him, she obeyed, eager to find out what he had in mind. He proceeded to undress her, his hands quick and sure as they removed each layer of clothing until she was naked in front of him.

Shooting her a mischievous look, he got on his knees. He leaned forward and kissed her neck. She closed her eyes and focused on his lips and his hands as they caressed her body. Her pulse raced as his fingers brushed her breasts and then her nipples, purposely teasing her. His thumb brushed her nipples which grew taut, and the ache between her legs increased, demanding that she find completion.

She whispered for him to touch her down there, and he lowered one of his hands. She wiggled to get closer to him as his fingers brushed her sensitive nub, but he didn't apply more pressure. She didn't know if she had the patience to wait. A part of her wanted to draw this out, to enjoy every caress. But another part, a more urgent part, insisted she climax now. She made another attempt to wiggle closer to him but he stopped her. She groaned in frustration, making him chuckle.

"It's only fair I tease you like you teased me," he murmured.

He lowered his head, kissing her as he went until his mouth reached her breasts. He kissed one and then the other while two of his fingers slid into her body. She arched her back and moaned. His tongue traced her nipple and he suckled lightly on it, an action that only served to make her more eager for him as he slipped a third finger into her. His thumb pressed firmly on her nub and worked in circular motions. She rocked her hips against him, desperately seeking out the climax that was within reach.

But he stopped stroking her with his thumb and stilled his fingers. She protested, but he ignored her and brought his head between her legs. Opening her eyes, she watched as his tongue went to her sensitive nub. She sharply inhaled and closed her eyes again. He resumed his stroking, his fingers working expertly inside her, rubbing the sensitive region deep in her core while his tongue went in lazy circular motions on her sensitive nub. She spread her legs further and rocked her hips in rhythm with him. Her body quickly built up toward the climax, and she grabbed his shoulders and told him to keep going. This time he didn't stop. She cried out as her orgasm came upon her, and she savored each wave of pleasure as it crashed into her.

Finally, when her body relaxed, his fingers left her body and he sat next to her. With a wicked smile, he pulled her onto his lap and entered her. She moaned in pleasure, her core still sensitive from her orgasm, and rocked her hips in time with his thrusting. There was no long build up to another climax this time. His actions were determined and focused, his thrusting taking her immediately to another climax, and as she cried out again, he grew taut and groaned while he released his seed into her.

Afterwards, she collapsed in his arms, and he held her tightly to him. He placed her hand on his chest where she could feel his heartbeat. She smiled and rested her head on his shoulder, content to rest in his embrace as she recalled how he told her that he loved her.

Chapter Twenty-Two

October

Claire's stomach rolled in protest at the thought of eating breakfast. She shivered and pushed the plate away from her. She couldn't even manage to eat fruit today. Glancing around the dining room to take her mind off the food, her gaze went to the large window and she smiled. Weston was a wonderful haven from the distractions of London, especially when she got to spend her time with her husband. And on this particular day, a nice ride on the estate might be a nice diversion. She'd walk if she had the energy, but expecting a child proved to be a tiring experience, and she spent more time reclining on her daybed instead of going for walks as she often did.

"Are you all right?" Nate asked.

"I'm fine." She turned her attention to him, noting his smile. "You're in a good mood."

His smile widened. "Why wouldn't I be? It's a gorgeous morning, and I get to spend it with my wife."

Her cheeks warmed at his words. "I have a surprise for you."

His eyebrows rose as he poked his fork into the last of his egg. "Oh?"

"Yes, but I won't tell you until we're at the pond."

"The pond?"

"Yes. It's a lovely place for a stroll, don't you think?"

He nodded and finished his food. "All right." He glanced at her plate. "You hardly ate anything."

"There's a good reason for that, but I want to tell you when we get to the pond."

He placed his napkin on the table and rose to his feet. "Are you ready?"

"Yes, I'm done," she said and joined him as he left the dining room.

"Are you going to give me any hints regarding your surprise?"

"If I did that, it wouldn't be a surprise."

Though he shook his head and let out an exasperated sigh, she noted his amusement. "And you say I'm stubborn."

She decided to ignore his comment and waited for the coachman to bring the carriage up to the house. Turning to Nate, she gave him a kiss on the cheek. "What I want to tell you is special, and I want the setting to be perfect. You wouldn't deny me that, would you?"

"No, I wouldn't," he admitted with a sly grin.

Her eyebrows furrowed. Did he suspect the truth? It wouldn't be much of a surprise if he did. Before she could give it any more thought, he led her out of the house and to the carriage.

On the way to the pond, he sat next to her and took her hand. "You look excited."

"That's because I am."

"What are you excited about?"

She opened her mouth to tell him but stopped when she realized his ploy. "You're not getting me to say anything until we get to the pond."

He grinned. "I had to try."

During the ride to the pond, he kissed her cheek and neck, making her giggle. "Nate, you're tickling me."

"Do you mind?" he whispered and nibbled her ear.

Tingles of delight raced up and down her spine. "No, but I didn't realize I was so ticklish."

"You weren't ticklish last night."

Blushing, she playfully shoved him away and straightened up as the carriage came to a stop. "You're a wicked man, Lord Roderick."

"Lord Roderick? Just a minute ago it was Nate."

She smiled at his teasing tone but turned her attention to the coachman when he opened the carriage door. After she got out, Nate told him they'd be back shortly and guided her down the path that led to a pond surrounded by a beautiful variety of trees with colorful leaves. She breathed in their sweet fragrance, thinking that few things were as perfect as enjoying a stroll with her husband in autumn.

"What a lovely sight," she said as she squeezed his arm in appreciation.

He stopped and faced her. "We're here, and I'm impatient. What do you have to tell me?"

She paused for a long moment and then broke into a grin. "I suppose I made you wait long enough. I'm expecting a child!"

His eyes lit up. "You are?"

She nodded. "The baby will be here in May."

He broke into a wide smile before he brought her into his arms and kissed her.

Wrapping her arms around his neck, she returned his kiss. Afterwards, she asked, "Did you know?"

"Would you be upset if I told you I suspected that's what you had to tell me?"

"No, I suppose not. But you're happy?"

"Very."

"That's all that matters."

Content, she put her arm around his and continued walking down the path with him. When she was done, they returned to the carriage.

As they rounded the bend that took them to the front entrance of the manor, she was surprised to see Perry's carriage. "Did you know your friend was coming this morning?" she asked Nate.

He stopped kissing her neck and peered out the window. "I knew he planned to stop by today, but he never said when. It's a good time. I can tell him the good news."

As their carriage pulled up behind Perry's, Claire realized Perry was standing by the butler who was waiting for them. "I don't think he's been waiting that long."

"No, but I wonder why he didn't bother going to the drawing room."

"Maybe he saw us coming and figured he'd wait outside. Besides, it's a sunny day. Maybe he wanted to enjoy the nice weather."

He shrugged. "Whatever the reason, it's good to see him. He owes me a game of chess."

"You aren't still upset you lost the last game, are you?"

"Don't be absurd. I'm not upset. I just want to make sure my strategy works, given the right circumstances."

"Whoever wins, I'm sure you'll have a good time."

The footman opened their door and Nate followed her out of the carriage.

Perry limped over to them and grinned. "Why Nate, I do believe you look happy today."

"That's because I'm going to win our next chess game," he replied.

"You know what I like most about you?" Perry began as he pointed his cane at him. "You never give up the hope that you'll win a game." Nate rolled his eyes, and Perry patted him on the shoulder. Turning to Claire, he said, "I was unnecessarily cruel. He does win a game every fifth time we play."

"Every fifth time?" he huffed.

"Maybe sixth." Perry shrugged. "I can't keep track."

Claire giggled.

"Do you have anything interesting to tell me?" Perry asked, looking expectantly between her and Nate.

Nate nodded. "I do, but have you found a wife yet?"

"I'm sorry to say not yet, but maybe next year during the Season, I'll find her. Let me venture a guess on your news. Claire is expecting a child?"

Claire sighed. "Why do I get the feeling everyone already knows about the baby?"

"You're an old married couple. What other news could you have?" Perry teased.

"You have to get accustomed to Perry," Nate told her. "He thinks he's funny. Sadly, no one else agrees."

"I don't know what you would do without each other," she said. "Let's go inside and have some tea. I'd like to hear how your ward is doing now that he's under your care again."

As they turned to go into the house, Perry said, "He's been much better. I don't know what you said to him, Claire, but he's not the same person I sent here. You must work miracles. First, my friend and then my ward... They're all better off since you came into their lives."

"Like I said, you're not that funny," Nate muttered, and despite his serious tone, Claire saw the twinkle in his eye.

Laughing, the three entered the drawing room.

***

July 1814
Weston

Claire ran to embrace her sister as Lilly and her husband got out of their carriage. "I'm so glad you came," Claire said as she pulled away from Lilly and examined her protruding belly. "When will you give birth?"

"In October."

"I'm so excited for you!"

"I am, too, and so is my husband" Lilly turned to Mister Morris. "He'll be a wonderful father."

Mister Morris wore a grin that went from ear to ear. "I hear you had a son," he told Claire.

"Yes. We named him Perry after my husband's friend." Claire motioned for Nate to join them. "Don't be shy, my lord."

Nate walked over to them, bouncing a happy boy in his arms. "I'm not shy. I just didn't want to interfere with two sisters hugging and laughing. It's good to see you, Mister Morris."

"It's an honor. This is a fine estate, Lord Roderick," Mister Morris said as he bowed.

Nate returned the gesture. "Thank you. Do you play chess?"

"Every chance I get."

"Then you won't mind playing a few games?"

"I'd be delighted."

Claire accepted her son from Nate who instructed the butler to take in their luggage.

"My housekeeper will show you to your rooms, and then I'll see how good you are at chess," Nate told Mister Morris. He glanced at Claire and Lilly. "Will you be coming inside?"

"We'll take a walk first," Claire replied. "We haven't seen each other for a while, and it'll be nice to find out everything that's happening in London."

He nodded and motioned for Mister Morris to join him and the butler.

Lilly accepted a reticule from the footman and rushed over to her. "I want to give you something that I hope will remind you of me. We haven't been able to see each other as much as we used to, but that doesn't mean I don't think of you often."

Touched by her words, she smiled and hugged Lilly again, careful not to make her son uncomfortable. "I've missed you."

"I've missed you, too, but we both married well, didn't we? Mother and Father are so proud."

"Yes, I suppose they are, but…"

"But what?"

"Did you marry Mister Morris because you wanted to or did you feel you had no other choice?"

Lilly put her arm around Claire's and led her down the path that would take them to the gazebo. Once they were out of earshot of anyone who might overhear them, she said, "I wanted to marry him. After that night we spied on Lord Hedwrett, I realized how much Lord Roderick loves you, and I decided I wanted the same kind of marriage you have. There was only one gentleman who loved me enough to stand up for me the way Lord Roderick stood up for you." She shrugged and smiled. "So I convinced Mister Morris to marry me."

"Convinced him?"

"It's a long story, but suffice it to say it took him a while to believe I'd be happy with him even though he didn't have a title." She opened her reticule and took out a cameo. "I had this engraved with my name, and I'm wearing a matching one with your name on it."

They stopped walking and Claire inspected the pretty profile of the young lady on the cameo. "It's lovely."

"This way, we can be with each other all the time."

"I like that." Perry fussed in her arms so Claire kissed his forehead. "I think he's getting tired."

"Oh, let me hold him!" Lilly held her arms out so Claire complied and handed him to her. She kissed his cheek and rubbed his back. "He looks a lot his father."

Claire giggled. "He's probably going to be a lot like his father, too. I caught Nate reading one of his boring books to him."

Lilly cringed. "One of his political books?"

"Yes."

"My poor nephew." She rocked him in her arms and sighed. "Thank goodness you have me. I'll make sure you get books that won't bore you." Lilly looked up from her nephew and added, "We're lucky to have our husbands, don't you think?"

"Yes, we are lucky."

"And, of course, they're lucky to have us."

Chuckling, Claire took her sister by the arm and nodded. "Yes, that's true, too."

The two sisters continued their walk to the gazebo, laughing and talking the whole way.

Coming Soon…

The Duchess of Watkins' husband just died, and her unscrupulous brother-in-law is ready to step in as the Duke of Watkins. In desperation, she enlists the help of the butler, and the two determine to quietly bury her husband and pretend he's still alive. It will be a secret they will keep to their graves in order to protect the estate.

After burying him in a forest in the middle of the night, they come across a man who's been beaten and left for dead. And this man happens to look just like her husband. Seeing this as the answer to their prayers, they take the man home in hopes he'll agree to be the new Duke of Watkins. There's only one problem. When he wakes up, he doesn't remember who he is, and a search for anyone who might know him leaves his true identity a mystery. Taking their chances, the Duchess of Watkins and the butler convince him he's her husband.

Unlike her first husband, this one is everything she's ever hoped for. But when he learns the truth, can he forgive her for her lie or will he go back to the life he had before?

Made in the USA
Middletown, DE
28 December 2021

57140747R00129